# BUM WING

## A Tale of Otherwise

# D.S. Sully

authorHOUSE®

AuthorHouse™
1663 Liberty Drive
Bloomington, IN 47403
www.authorhouse.com
Phone: 1-800-839-8640

Published by AuthorHouse    03/18/2013

ISBN: 978-1-4817-1855-4 (sc)
ISBN: 978-1-4817-1854-7 (hc)
ISBN: 978-1-4817-1853-0 (e)

Library of Congress Control Number: 2013903158

# Contents

# Acknowledgments

 his book is dedicated to the memory of my youngest brother, Scott, who I especially miss whenever it comes time to cast a fishing line, start a campfire, or zoom around with nieces Alyssa, Emily, or Carly in a golf cart.

Also to be acknowledged is Hua-Yao Tung, whose artwork "Golden Owl" graces the front cover.

# Introduction

 ometimes I feel like a full-fledged misfit. Perhaps, I really am just that. When this situation becomes far too much for me to handle, there is fortunately a place to go. It's a secret hideout, located deep in the woods behind my Grandpa's home. This haven is by no means an ordinary forest, yet instead, it whimsically sprawls about as woodlands of jutting bluffs, deep hollows, twisting waterways, and elderly trees. What become scary at times are the haunting echoes, peculiar tracks, and shadowy movements which accent this enclave. Most of these occurrences are due to the strange critters who reside within here. And they, by the way, are curiously and confoundedly, the basis of this story.

What seems most interesting about these resident critters is that so many are just like me. Perhaps that is why I spend hour after hour in their domain. By venturing into these woods, I am not running away from anything or anyone, yet learning instead that I am not so different after all. It is these woods and its critters who are teaching me this lesson on being otherwise.

Be mindful that these critters I am referring too are not just the furry, feathery, crawly, or scaly types. Some are two-legged and walk upright like me. Although most are quite friendly, each and every one of them is ever so mysterious. This equally applies to the deep-rooted inhabitants, such as raggedy oaks and zombie timbers. They too are stealthy critters in these woods as well.

At first, most of these critters kept their distance from me. Over time, we slowly but surely got acquainted. Because I have now become one of them, they no longer shy away from me. Having formed a kinship among us, we critters seem to understand each other quite well. However, outside these trusty woods, far too many others do not always view us fairly or treat us kindly. In hopes of changing that reality once and for all, I now need to share this tale of otherwise which involves an elusive dwarf Indian, a moonshiner's granddaughter, a wandering war-torn monk, a gadabout granddad, a duo of boar hunting barons, a bystander buzzard, and most of all, a wise old owl shouldering a bum wing.

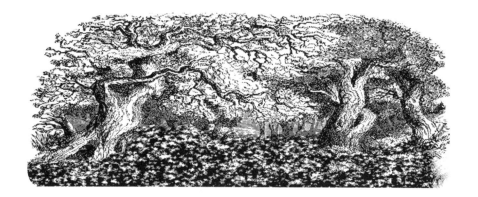

# STUMPED

---

*You need not fly in order to soar.*

---

pon getting off this old yellow bus today, I am not sure of ever going back to school again. Always being picked on by that nasty bonehead numbskull kid named Boone is driving me crazy. Boone is a goon. He has got to be the biggest jerk at my school. And because of my unique situation, I get to be his target each and every school day.

Because the town I live in is quite small, sticking out like a sore thumb oftentimes becomes routine. This so happens to be my misfortune. In some ways, I have become the local Charlie Brown without any Snoopy for a sidekick. It's a frustrating and confusing predicament that sometimes makes me more determined and other times downtrodden.

There are days when I wonder why I wasn't born to be like other kids. Despite all the doctors and counselors who have analyzed, scrutinized, and examined me, no one has any clear answers as to what can be done about my one leg being considerably shorter than the other. As a result, I wobble and weave whenever walking about. It is just the lopsided way I am and will always be. For the most part, this would not be such an ongoing dilemma if not for unrelenting bullies like Boone.

Adding to this predicament is the fact that my given name is Elmore Vonvanderen. Although most of my friends just call me Vandy, some classmates like to make fun of my first name. Christened after my great-great grandfather, I agree that it is an odd sort of name and sounds like Elmer. As such, morons like Boone enjoy referring to me as the blundering cartoon character, Elmer Fudd and asking me if I have recently chased after any "wascally wabbits".

Today Boone decided to label me Igor. According to this butthead, I walk about like the creepy lab assistant in *Frankenstein*. Boone even took it upon himself to now follow behind me in the hallway, as if he were the freakish monster, and then repeatedly cry out ghoulishly, "Help me Igor. Help me Igor". Unfortunately, there were some bystander kids who actually thought this was really funny. Those who did not like what Boone was doing said nothing, for dreaded fear of becoming his next chosen target and being picked on as well. Boone however, is not my only lingering problem. Ever since my classmates began watching the popular television show, *Gunsmoke*, some now refer to me as Chester, because of the limping deputy sheriff in this western series.

Nobody ever needs to remind me that I walk in a goofy manner. If I try to run at a fast pace, I just get out of balance and go tumbling to the ground. For this reason, I sometimes get chased by the mean kids, who hope to see me dash and crash. During my grade school days, teachers banned me from playground games such as Red Rover and Pom-Pom Pullaway. Because of this haphazard reality, sports have become off-limits for me. Even though I am pretty good at shooting free throws, the process of dribbling, rebounding, and all the other maneuvers of basketball keep me off the hardwood court. With football and baseball, it is pretty much the same sort of misfit. Still, there is a part of me wanting to be an athlete and avid competitor. When I attempt to get involved in gym classes, my teachers always seem so afraid of me getting injured. What really hurts however, is not being part of the action.

After being rejected from sports participation, I decided this year to try out for the school play. Although I was willing to take on just about any role, I overheard two of my teachers discussing how I would be a distraction in the cast. One teacher even feared that I might stumble and then tumble, right off the front of the stage. As such, I got put in charge of drawing the curtains. How do you suppose they would respond if I wanted to add my offbeat steps to the school's marching band? It is really hard to put your best foot forward when others consider it off kilter.

When it comes to being different, I am well aware of this situation. It often scares me to think how those who are visibly unlike others around here, become the talk of the town. For example, there are two local gals who get gossiped about all the time. One is the hunchback woman who works at Crubaugh's Bakery, and the other is the mustached lady, at Perkins IGA grocery. Although respected as a policeman, rotund Officer Tiny gets to be the subject of the local tongue wagging as well. And of course, everyone passing by George's junkyard on the way to St. Joseph's Church always confess their thoughts about his eccentric ways. Hearing what people have to say concerning these neighbors, makes me wonder as to what is said pertaining to me. Grandpa once told me that even though all of us are created equal, it just seems that some folks are viewed as more equal than others.

Realizing that others get picked on as well, doesn't really cause me to shrug off the mean-spirited name calling or the mimicking of my not so level locomotion. I keep saying to myself that none of us are perfect, but that does not help either. If not for my grandfather to talk with, this life of mine would be miserable.

After losing my parents to an auto accident four years ago, I moved out to the countryside and began living with my maternal grandparents. Just a year ago, Grandma Dottie passed away after a heart ailment. She got called "Polka Dot" based on her love of dancing. Because my paternal grandparents reside in another state, I do not see them very often. Aside from a few remaining relatives in this area, it is pretty much up to Grandpa and I to look out for each other. As a widower, Grandpa seems to know how I feel. Though a bit cranky at times, he is the most important person in the world to me. My mother use to refer to him as the family's wise old owl.

Before retiring several years ago, Grandpa was a long time road builder. He operated graders, bulldozers, backhoes, and those huge dump trucks. As such, he claims to have driven and fixed every road in this county. When not working the roads, Grandpa had an unusual endeavor. Every autumn, Grandpa became fondly known as "Nutter", by wandering the area woods and collecting walnuts, hickory nuts, butternuts, hazelnuts, and chestnuts. In the springtime, he would plant nut tree seedlings

throughout this neck of the woods. Basically, my grandfather represented a nutty version of the folklore character, Johnny Appleseed. When I asked Grandpa why he goes about planting trees, he told me that doing so was repayment for all the tall timbers knocked down during his road building days. "And besides," Grandpa said, "I'm nuts about nuts."

Always carried by Grandpa was an old hickory hiking stick, used not only for balance on uneven ground, yet also to knock nuts and fruits off tree branches. Now hobbled by severe arthritis in both his knees and hips, he rarely ventures about anymore. Nonetheless, the nickname "Nutter" is what most local folks still call him. On my last birthday, he handed me his varnished hickory stick and proclaimed that I now must become the main scout of the woods. To others, this sturdy and crooked staff may look like nothing more than an old branch, yet it has become one of my most cherished possessions. Upon venturing into the woods, it is my trusted companion to steady my steps and ward off imaginary trolls, menacing beasts, and bewitching things.

Whenever Grandpa Nutter senses that I have had a really bad day, his advice is always the same. In a gravelly voice and pretending to be gruff, he bellows out to me, "You need to take a hike young man!" This is grandfather's guiding way of telling me to head into the woods. According to his wise old owl senses, a little solitude in the forest can cure almost anything. He is usually right, and that is why today, I am going to heed the advice of this grey bearded wiseman.

The dense woods bordering my home are no ordinary patches of scattered saplings, elderly oaks, and tangled shrubs. This sprawling landscape of shadowy hollows, twisted timbers, and jutting bluffs was once labored upon by my ancestors, who attempted to convert it into harvested fields and lucrative lead ore mines. However, the combination of what are now abandoned farmsteads and leftover mining sites has been transformed into an immense state park. What years ago had been perceived as a new start for sod-busting civilization has now reversed into a place of conservation. To a kid like me, this is simply a refuge of secret places.

The namesake for the park is the region's first territorial governor, who acquired this post after staking mining claims to everything he could in these parts. This expansive park attracts lot of adventurers looking for a walk on the wild side. Comprising thousands of acres, this rural setting includes woodlands, wetlands, meadowlands, and fallow croplands. It also hosts a manmade lake, another lake currently under construction, lookout knolls, beaver and muskrat bogs, leftover logging roads from the Pinery era, and remnants of the hardscrabble pioneer farms. According to my science teacher, this region was untouched by the prehistoric glaciers and thus known as the Driftless Area. My teacher also said this countryside once consisted of prairies with roaming herds of buffalo and elk. Supposedly, the last bison was shot in 1832 and elk in 1868. When roaming about this landscape, I sometimes imagined discovering one of these long lost creatures.

Though many outsiders come here to hike the hilly trails and fish the clear waters, there are secluded places and hidden treasures concealed within this rural park, known only to intrusive locals like me. Protected by barriers of briar thickets, nettle patches, and buckthorn, these destinies are avoided by all but the bravest, who dare to seek and discover. For example, in some of the ravines lie makeshift junkyards, where vintage farm machines and castoff belongings were conveniently discarded years ago. Old timers around here refer to these dump-off ditches as "washes". Marooned in one of the canyons is a broken-down Model T Ford, forever becoming a rusted part of these hallowed grounds. Beyond salvage, the spoke wheels of this neglected metal geezer are hopelessly sunk well into the earth. It is a mystery car, perhaps abandoned decades ago by a

bank robber or bootlegger, while the cops were in hot pursuit. I like to believe that it is somehow connected to one of the infamous mobsters such as John Dillinger or Al Capone, who oftentimes ventured into this state when things got a little too hot in Chicago. Or maybe, this age-old auto simply got stolen as a joyride from a nearby farm. It almost seems impossible that this vehicle got driven to such a secluded location and became sadly orphaned. Imprisoned by all the trees and brush now grown around it, this four-wheeled elder has settled into its eternal resting place and can never leave. Sometimes I wonder whether anyone besides me or Grandpa, knows about this spooky jalopy. I also wonder as to whether this vehicle could also be haunted with the spirit of its driver still seated behind the steering wheel.

Poking about the scrap heaps with my hickory stick, I've discovered cracked whiskey jugs and pickle crocks, canning jars, blue medicine bottles, tobacco and coffee tins, busted chairs, dented kettles, syrup and molasses containers, injured tin toys, leaky buckets and wash tubs, milk cans, giant horseshoes, axe heads, iron wheels with busted spokes, broken pitch forks, bent tools, tractor parts, a treadle sewing machine, rolls of barbed wire, farm implements, and all kinds of other quirky things from the distant past. I even started a collection of clanging cowbells after finding several of them within the trash troves. Every once in a while, exposed among the refuse and rubble are the discarded bones of some bygone creature, which most likely were deceased Holsteins associated with the cowbells.

Sometimes, I envision myself as an undaunted detective. What may appear as garbage to others, are revealing clues to me. Although often smashed and trashed, I consider these telltale things as fragments of time. Each trip into these woods begins another secretive search. However, one element of my quests continues to elude me. In scouring this landscape, I have yet to discover any of the old root cellars, covered over and left behind when the pioneer farmsteads were torn down. Imagine what lies buried within them. Perhaps hidden inside these earthen storerooms, there are ancient weapons and other artifacts. It sure would be cool to find at least one of these tombs.

Being a rock hound and bone hunter, I've tried scavenging for precious metals, gemstones, and fossils. To this point, the only outcome has been some pieces of quartz and a lead nugget. One of these days, I am bound to unearth the skeletal remains of a wooly mammoth or some other ancient monster.

As part of my search, I routinely scout for old wagon trails and logging roads. Most are now camouflaged by the resurgence of underbrush and saplings. By studying these woods carefully, you can detect these ribbons of smaller growth winding through the taller trees and over the ridges. There are also clues such as the earth-etched ruts remaining from when the ground was soft and the wagon loads were heavy. As another clue, any huge flat stump betrays where journeying lumberjacks cross cut into the woods. Following these once beaten paths, you may even stumble upon an old foundation, marked by rocks, rubble, rotting beams, and even a few relics.

Throughout the area's numerous sandstone ridges there are all kinds of ledges and rock outcroppings. Oftentimes when exploring these places, I daydream about how the native peoples of long ago would have sought shelter in such hideaways. Along the narrow ledges, I have even found arrowheads. Sometimes this is where I see the most unusual tracks such as paw prints with protruding claws. Grandpa kiddingly likes to warn me to be on the lookout for any footprints baring six toes, for this means that forest trolls are trudging about. What often worries me, are not trolls, but rather the risky chance of discovering a coiled timber rattler in the stony havens. Even though I have never encountered one of these poisonous vipers, I know they exist because of a local snake hunter named Woody. This kooky guy searches the ridges for rattlers and then brings them into town to show off at the farmer's market. Although the Timber Rattlers garner the most attention, Woody sometimes brings along Bull snakes, Browns snakes, and an occasional Eastern Hognose. After scouring the marshy bottom lands near the river, Woody captures local swamp rattlers known as Massasauga. In Chippewa language, this name means "huge river mouth". What Woody does with any of these snakes afterwards, nobody seems to know.

Grandpa Nutter once told me that in years past, heavy rains often flooded dens and caused waves of rattlers to emerge. Panicked locals referred to this spectacle as a snake stampede. As such, the county put a cash bounty on rattlers. This resulted in a snake posse scouring the countryside and almost wiping out the entire venomous varmint population. Nowadays, Woody seems to be the only one who can find any remaining rattlesnakes. While most folks are okay with an absence of these slithering reptiles, I am not sure rooting out all the rattlers is a good idea.

To hike this rustic area and reach the woods, you often need to cross through overgrown fields. Although far from being the spooky nature of the shadowy woods, these fields are menaced by thistle giants with purple heads and grisly arms. Growing wild and untamed, you must tread carefully when approaching them. During chance encounters with these weed bullies, a battle often ensues. Raising my trusty hiking staff and taking a precise swing, I have lopped off more than one head of these monsters. In similar battles, I have also flailed my walking stick at another nemesis, the Red-winged blackbird. Just as harrowing as the thistle creeps, yet tinier and more mobile, these blackbirds will fearlessly dive bomb any trespassers near their nests. Last summer, one of these frantic-flying maniacs, actually knocked the hat right off my head. I narrowly escaped before having my scalp pierced and eyes plucked out. No matter what path is chosen, you always tread cautiously in this realm.

Now being reclaimed by tall grass and scrub brush, these bygone farm fields use to represent waves of grain. Though corn, oats, and alfalfa are commonplace around the remaining farms here today, it was mainly wheat which got cultivated and harvested by the early settlers. In fact, so much wheat got grown that it eventually depleted the soils and thus required other crops to be planted, one of which was tobacco. I use to think that tobacco was only a Dixieland crop from the South. However, my Uncle Homer once told me, that because of the area's tobacco crops, the Ben Franklin Five & Dime store in town use to serve as a cigar factory. I guess this all goes to show just how many changes both your hometown and the woods in your back yard have gone through. Maybe that is why I keep on exploring the park nearby.

Those wandering the marked trails of these woods, get to marvel in Mother Nature by visiting spots such as Thomas' Cave, Twin Valley, Enee Point, Halverson ponds, and Stephens' Falls, Then again, there are some like me, who venture from the beaten paths, to explore other caves and waterfalls, remnants of mining digs, freakish trees, weird tracks, suspicious dens, strange rock formations, and clandestine critters, that most others will never meet. And sometimes, there are even characters within these woods, who are likewise, and otherwise, the same as me.

What's really best about these woods, are the sights and sounds which help me to think about things in my life. Sometimes I come here to remember my parents and question why they had to die so young. Other times, I sit at my secret ledge and ponder why I am not like most Kids. Today however, I am going to my favorite spot just to be as far away as I can from bullies like Boone.

Starting out with my trusty hiking stick in hand, I headed as usual to my cherished lookout bluff. It is about a hundred yards from one of the marked hiking trails, yet cannot be seen because of the trees and rocks concealing it. From a protruding ledge, I can view the valley below me while remaining hidden from anyone or anything else. This vantage point is like a theater box seat overlooking a wild cast of characters. At times, I watch deer, possums, skunks, foxes, squirrels, raccoons, rabbits, chipmunks, woodchucks, and even a weasel or two passing through. On one occasion, I even caught a glimpse of the sneaky bobcat that resides here and quietly prowls about. About the only thing I have yet to capture sight of is a wily badger. Then again, there are likely other strange critters which have eluded me as well. And although I cannot prove it, there has got to be at least one bear in these woods.

Grandpa taught me that by barging into the woods, most folks rarely see the creatures which reside within. When you merely wander through the woods, the critters will usually see you first and then scatter. However, if you seek out a good hideaway spot to nestle into it, sit quietly and ever so still, eventually the woods will come alive all around you. That's just what I do and it really works. Of course, this is dependent on not being seen and exposed by the jabber-jawed crows, who will signal your presence by squawking away. As forest sentries, these loudmouthed crows can be used to my advantage as well, by letting me know whenever something or someone is approaching. The forests and fields have all kinds of signs and signals to teach you.

What I have learned mostly about are the sounds. Sometimes when leaning back against a tree and closing my eyes, I hear more than I can actually see in these woods. A drum beating on the ridge means a ruffed grouse is nearby. Scolding chatter from the treetops denotes an irritated squirrel. A chirping alarm signifies a chipmunk on sentry. Rustling leaves on the forest floor betray foraging possums and raccoons. Snapping twigs warn of large predators on the hunt. Frantic hammering indicates a woodpecker hard at work. A soft and muted footstep translates into a wary deer edging its way along a game trail. Distant mooing serves as a reminder that dairy farms border this park.

Listening to the sky, you will also witness it talking. Shrill whistling in the air announces that mourning doves are rocketing about. Haunting screeches from overhead designates the presence of a hovering red tail hawk. Should honking emerge from overhead, a change of seasons is being forecast by migrating geese. If restless winds begin to blow, the elderly oaks anxiously voice their creaking opinions. Being more discrete, the swaying tall pines choose to whisper their viewpoints.

The tranquility of these natural sounds can oftentimes be interrupted by heavily trudging footsteps, which almost always end up being manmade. Sometimes, there are also howls, growls, hoots, and hubbubs down in the hollow, which create mysteries as well.

Considering myself a forest sleuth, I try to take in all the sights and sounds around me. During this day's venture, instead of spying on the critters, I got fixated on a lone decaying stump, blocking part of my view. As a broken off tree trunk with all of its branches and a lot of bark withered away, this stump stood about six and a half feet high. Weathered and naked, holes were poked into it by rampaging woodpeckers. Its hollow nature was exposed by the small opening at the base of this old timber. Stripped of any identity, it seemed almost impossible to tell what kind of majestic tree it had once been.

Still upset over the most recent confrontation with Boone, I decided to take out my frustrations on this forlorn stump. Climbing down from the ledge, I hiked over to this dead timber. With a close-up inspection of its decaying roots, it seemed amazing to me that this thing had stubbornly remained upright. However, I now planned to change all that.

Due to the stump's rotten disposition, I christened it "Boone". With this said, I then proclaimed to the woods as my witness, "Boone, it is time for you to go down." Leaning my right shoulder against the sorry structure, I expected some kind of resistance. Instead, the roots easily gave way and this ancient tree began tilting. Digging in my heels for more leverage, I placed both hands on the lopped off trunk and shoved with all my might. Dictating a forthcoming demise with a decree of "Timber!", the stump forfeited its stance and descended before me. Upon hitting the ground, it shattered into splinters. Pieces of wood flew everywhere. What then happened next was totally unexpected. In the midst of this destruction, an enormous ball of feathers rolled across the forest floor. Finally coming to a stop, this stunned critter lay motionless on its back. Wings with long brown-striped feathers sprawled out from each side. Because of its sheer size, piercing yellow eyes, and white throat patch, I could tell right away that this was a Great Horned owl. A huge hooked beak and foreboding talons added to its menacing look and magnificence. And of course, atop its head were those tuffs, which Grandpa Nutter once taught me were actually just feathers and not ears or horns.

With feathers severely ruffled, this bird of prey began recovering from its' daze by shaking his head. Regaining his footing and senses, the owl slowly stood up and shook its head back and forth. While doing so, he caught sight of me staring down at him. Amidst this eye to eye faceoff, there next came something totally unexpected. "Are you the scoundrel responsible for all this?" said the owl. Rather than reply, I sort of froze still for the moment and kept on staring. Again and in a much louder tone of voice, the owl shouted out, "Answer me. Why in tarnation did you destroy my home?" This time I responded back, "How come you

are talking to me?" Sounding even more miffed, the owl then quickly retorted, "Because you obviously are the one who wrecked my home!" In turn I noted, "No, that is not what I meant. I was just asking how it is that you can speak?" Seeming annoyed by my question, the owl hesitated a bit and then remarked, "What is so peculiar about a bird being able to talk. Many of us are quite articulate and somewhat bilingual. Parrots mouth off all too often. Parakeets, cockatiels, and macaws just don't know when to shut up. Mockingbirds always have something to say. Certain doves seem to mourn all day long. Cuckoos babble to no end. Loons usually sound loony. And most crows can't refrain from brainless squawking. As for me, I have always been able to speak and happen to be fluent in many languages, including yours. I suppose you fully expected a traditional run-of-the-mill hoot or two."

As ever so magical as these woods have always been to me, I never imagined such an unbelievable moment. Whoever or whatever this jabbering owl was, I now found myself conversing with a more than mysterious critter. Perhaps Boone had really driven me crazy after all and this was the result. Although everything around me felt like a farfetched dream, this communicating owl standing before me would just not go away.

"Now that I am homeless, what are you going to do about it? And furthermore," demanded the owl, "who the heck are you anyway and what are you doing down here in my territory?" Before I could even answer, the owl gave me an inquisitive look and began rattling on once again. "Wait a minute," said the owl. "Now I know what this is all about. Yes I most certainly do. You are that leaning boy from the latest vision that Tustis told me of. I can definitely tell just by the way you are standing."

Based on what this baffling critter had just blabbered to me, I had a whole lot of questions to ask of my own. I first needed to find out who this Tustis was and what this curious thing about a leaning boy meant. With my inquiries thus made, this feathered character began revealing to me some intriguing tales. He started by noting that most here in these woods refer to him as "Sage". According to his friend Tustis, he is a rare breed of bird bestowed with the title of "Earth Owl". As for commenting on Tustis, the only thing that Sage would tell me is that I soon would meet this friend of his and learn much more. However, Sage did go on to mention that Tustis had a recent vision of this current encounter, which included a falling tree, rolling owl, leaning boy, and future endeavor. When I asked Sage what this future endeavor involved, he just shrugged and said that this part of the vision was not yet clear to him or Tustis.

Before I could ask another question, Sage insisted that it was my turn to explain myself. I complied by saying that most of my friends call me Vandy, yet there were some who tease me about my real name or the way I walk. And though I rarely talk to anyone about these personal concerns, I then began explaining to Sage, the calamity of my life with uneven legs and unwanted attention. My grumbling next included being left out of sports and other routine kids' stuff. I even told him how bad I sometimes feel about not going to dances and my fears that no girl would want to go on a date with me. Then, I ended my sob story by noting the continuous problems I was having with dirtbag Boone.

All of this seemed so weird. Here I was talking to a strange woodland critter and sharing details that I had not even mentioned to Grandpa Nutter. During this exchange, Sage just sat intently listening. When I finally finished, he sort of cocked back his head and said, "Sounds to me like we are birds of a feather and two of a kind. Just like you, I have had

a hurdle to overcome. I've got this bum wing which keeps me from flying. As a fledging leaving the nest, it got seriously injured. Although my left wing works fine, the right wing can only be lifted ever so slightly and does not flap quite well. In desperation, I can become airborne only momentarily by vigorously shaking my left wing and straining the right one. Anyhow, that would require all my strength and possibly lead to further injury. According to Tustis, my particular situation makes me an Earth Owl, both grounded and gifted. I too get teased at times, especially by the obnoxious crows, who chase me, taunt me, and call me Wingding. Through it all, I have learned to adapt and be distinguished as otherwise. And not everyone can make that claim."

What Sage had just shared with me, raised my curiosity. "What do you mean by that phrase, distinguished as otherwise?" I asked. In response, Sage opened his eyes widely and seemed to smirk. "It is like this," he said. "There are those with two wings to fly and those who are otherwise. There are also those who see, hear, and speak perfectly well, and those who are otherwise. Then again, there are those who move about with considerable ease and those who are otherwise. And just as notable, there are those whose shapes, sizes, and actions are similar, and those who are otherwise. Some refer to these things as differences or disabilities, yet I instead perceive them as abilities and attributes that are considerably and most honorably, otherwise. And here in these very woods, there are by far, many of us who are indeed otherwise, some of whom you will soon meet such as Tustis, Brother Oliver, Sadie, and perhaps even old Buzz. However, before any and all of this occurs, you must first help me to find a new residence."

Looking at Sage in the midst of his destroyed home, I felt terrible. Because of my aggression, I had more or less become the same kind of bully as Boone. I began apologizing to Sage and pledging to immediately create for him a lean-to as a temporary shelter, something I had learned from my dad during a camp outing. While gathering nearby branches and beginning the construction process, Sage shared with me that the old stump was ready to fall anyway, and that he had actually been thinking about seeking out a new home. His next idea then caught me off-guard.

Sage told me that not far from this spot, an old lead ore mine remained hidden. After being abandoned, its entrance got covered up with rocks and debris. With my help and a miner's pick, Sage assured me it could be re-opened to become his new home. Being this was Saturday and getting late in the day, I agreed to come back the following morning and complete the task at hand. As I finished the lean-to in the diminishing daylight, I bid Sage farewell and headed home. Bursting inside from all that had been encountered today, I knew this eventful outing needed to be kept secret for now, even from Grandpa Nutter.

Upon awakening the next day at sunrise, I quickly dressed and quietly snuck into grandfather's tool shed. Finding the long pointed pick that would be needed, I headed to the woods as fast as possible, before Grandpa Nutter or anyone else could spot me. I knew that if any of the park rangers were out and about, they would not take kindly to me entering their domain with any sort of excavating tool. When I arrived at the makeshift lean-to, Sage was ready and waiting. He then escorted me to an area just north of my lookout ledge.

As we hiked along a sloping ridge, I felt the strange sense of being followed. Looking back over my right shoulder, all I could see was a blue jay perched in a nearby tree. While continuing to walk behind Sage, I looked back several more times to again see this same blue feathered bird flying from tree to tree and remaining close by. Finally, I stopped and asked Sage as to whether we were being followed by this blue jay. "Of course we are," Sage replied. "That's my friend Snitch. He watches over me and lets me know everything that is going on in these woods. From time to time, he is also my courier whenever I need to send out messages. Don't worry. He is keeping a lookout for both of us."

With this distraction settled, I stopped looking back and continued following Sage up a fairly steep grade. On the side of the hill and behind a clump of birch trees, was a mound of large and small rocks. "Behind these rocks," said Sage, "is a dug out shaft once belonging to a miner and moonshiner named Henry. When this mine turned out not to have enough ore, Henry used it as a hideaway storehouse

for his bootlegging business. Having never been in there, I am not sure what was left behind."

There seemed no reason to doubt Sage about this mine site. Grandpa Nutter claimed that there are leftover shafts throughout this entire area. Even in town, there are tunnels winding beneath the streets and buildings. The historic county courthouse sits above a network of these twisting tunnels. Not long ago, mine shafts caused two of the town's streets to cave in during road work. Down in Dirty Hollow, a local swimming hole called Crystal Lake suddenly disappeared forever when it drained into the ore mines beneath it. My dad once told me that he and his friends use to climb into these excavations and explore them. As a safety measure, these vintage mines got blocked off and filled in.

After beginning to pull the stones out, one by one, I asked Sage how he came to know of this hidden mine. Sage then noted how a friend named Sadie, showed him this secret place. As the mine owner's granddaughter, Sadie once helped to block off this abandoned claim. According to Sage, this lady called Sadie was someone I was also destined to meet.

While continuing to dig and lift away stones, I wondered just who these Tustis and Sadie characters were that Sage kept referring to. Would they be as unique as this owl or perhaps even more peculiar? Before I had a chance to ask, an opening suddenly appeared upon dislodging the next stone. After rolling aside several more, there was now an entrance with just a big enough space for me to crawl through. Needing more light for seeing inside, I had to again commence pulling away a few more hefty boulders to enlarge the entrance. If valuable treasures lay within, I wanted to be the first to discover them.

Right away, I could tell that this was not a huge or deep mine shaft. Instead, it consisted of a small chamber which the local old timers often call "badger holes". When recalling stories about the mining era, Grandpa Nutter said that many of the prospectors were known as "Badgers", because they both worked and lived in these dug out burrows.

Poking my head and shoulders through the entrance, a strong whiff of musty air touched my face. Straining in the faint light that now filtered to the back of this cavern, I spotted several clay jugs, a rusted pail, and a kerosene lantern. What really caught my eyes however, were three strange symbols appearing starkly on the sandstone walls of this mine. As best as I could tell, the first drawing depicted a bird-like face. The second one silhouetted a spooky figure. The third and farthest from me, seemed to be some kind of animal track. Feeling a bit freaked out by all this, I backed out of the mine shaft and began noting to Sage what I saw inside. Appearing perplexed, Sage then wandered in and decided to take a close-up look for himself.

Following some considerable review, Sage finally exited the mine. "Not being quite what I anticipated, this will do fine as a home for me," said Sage. "While somewhat surprised by the furnishings, I sort of like the added artwork. However, my friend Tustis will need to see these markings and tell me what they symbolize. In the meantime, tell no one of this place. I will send word to Tustis by way of Snitch. We will meet at this time next week and perhaps there will then be answers. As for now, I must begin setting up home."

With this said, it became obvious to me of Sage needing time to himself and that I should be on my way. Along the return route, I kept thinking of Sage and wondering about future encounters with Tustis, Sadie, and any others. Being careful again not to be seen walking through these woods with a pick, I luckily made it back to my home without Grandpa Nutter or anyone else encountering me. Still, keeping all this from grandpa would be a challenge like no other for me.

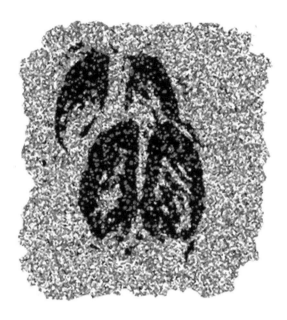

Throughout Sunday night, I remained restless and had a hard time getting to sleep. While sharing breakfast with Grandpa the next morning, a nervous feeling kept me wondering on whether to tell him that I had met a talking owl. As the Monday school bus approached, I waited while still thinking about all the events of this past weekend. Now held within me were secrets that I so desperately wanted to share with my schoolmates, yet dared not to do so. In some ways, I even felt eager about getting to school. Meeting Sage, not only made me feel important, yet more courageous as well. The advice he had given me toward dealing with Boone, would now be put to the test.

According to Sage, I needed a better strategy when it came to bullies. I know that talking to teachers, counselors, and other adults is the right thing to do, but this never seems to work for me. Just trying to ignore the ridicule does not work either. Instead of always walking away and feeling defeated by someone like Boone, I needed to face him and follow through. So here was the plan. The next time that Boone begins his harassment, I will look him in the eye and respond with the following. "If you like so much to pick on me, then you must like having me around. Therefore, whenever you get on my case, I will now become your shadow and follow you about. And if you try to beat me up, so be it, because that will lead to you being expelled and me not having to deal with you anymore."

Confronting a bully is risky business, yet doing nothing about it is even more hazardous. Based on Sage's theory however, most bullies don't know how to handle someone who dares to walk along with them, rather than away from these jerks. In my case, doing so might just be enough to freak out Boone and turn the tide. As the bus now entered the school parking lot, my stomach was churning and nerves on edge with the prospects of what would happen today. It did not take long to find out.

The moment I walked through the entryway and stepped into the main corridor, there was Boone staring me down. Without hesitation, he again started with the "Igor" routine. Gathering up all the courage possible, I slowed my pace and angled toward him. In the midst of his next sentence, I cut him off and began my dialogue. Boone seemed dumbfounded. His pea-brain did not know how to respond. Seeing that I was not going anywhere, he started fidgeting. Finally, Boone just muttered out "Bug off" and treaded away.

For now, I had gotten a reprieve. Although I knew this was no guarantee that Boone or any others would cease forever from picking on me, I just had to enjoy the moment and savor this victory of sorts. Even though my ongoing stance was somewhat off-kilter, Sage had now taugt me how to really stand on my own two feet. As the rest of the week went on, I kept thinking about the confidence I had gained, what had been learned, and what was to come, all due to an encounter with a most mysterious and unusual owl.

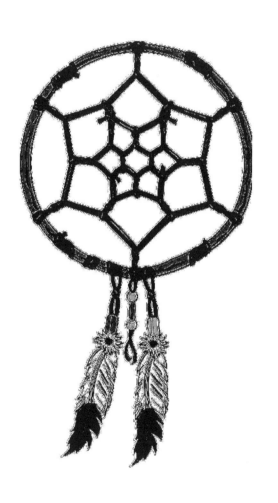

# SMALL WONDER

---

*Those who are less than perfect are more than gifted.*

---

ost, who know Grandpa Nutter, are well aware of his gifted storytelling skills. As a young boy, I got to hear all his renditions of local folktales involving the Ridgeway Phantom, Scotch Giant, Archibald the Hermit, the Hobos of Dirty Hollow, and Bachelor Jack. He also has an intriguing story about three girls named Alyssa, Emily, and Carly, who have a magical encounter with an enchanting critter called the "Beavcoon". Without a doubt, grandpa's scariest tale relates to the "Swampees", those strange amphibious people who live near the backwater sloughs of the river and have faces like catfish.

My favorite tale has always been the one about the Elf Indian. Several generations ago, the local folks around here caught occasional glimpses of a dwarf-sized Indian roaming about. As word spread of this small wonder, Barnum and Bailey sent an agent from its circus company to set up a nearby camp and issue a bounty for the capture of this elusive little man. Wanting to prevail in a bitter rivalry with the competing Ringling Brothers, Barnum and Bailey viewed this mystifying Indian as an added gold mine for their world famous freak show. There had already been a character from this neck of the woods, who got persuaded into joining the circus as the seven-foot three inch Scotch Giant. Just like this behemoth, the impish Indian held the promise of attracting huge crowds. There was even speculation about this character joining Buffalo Bill's Wild West Show.

Despite all the attempts made by a horde of anxious bounty hunters, no one was able to even catch sight of this Indian. Even with the best of hounds, he could not be tracked down. According to local folklore, this Indian had the ability to suddenly disappear like a ghost. Some also claimed him to be a shape shifter who could change into an animal form such as a wolf, bear, eagle or owl. Eventually the bounty on this mysterious character was withdrawn and the manhunt ceased. Since then and even to this day, folks continue to catch distant glimpses of what appears to be a smallish Indian man wandering the area woods.

Whenever I hike into the woods, I often imagine myself encountering this legendary Indian. This is just a kid's fantasy within the magic of the forest. As believable as Grandpa Nutter could make his stories, they were crafted to be more entertaining than truthful. At least, that is what I thought until this day.

It had been a week since my introduction to Sage. While now wandering into the woods for another meeting with this outlandish owl, I kept wondering whether the events of last weekend had really happened. Along the way, I spotted a decaying tree, somewhat similar to the stump I had previously toppled. Because of the large hole, midway up its trunk, this tree appeared to be hollow. However, it was much larger than the stump and had many of its branches still remaining. This time, instead of trying to knock this tree over, I stretched myself upward to peer into the hollow cavity. Surprisingly, I got stared back at by several pairs of eyes. This tree was home to a family of raccoons, who snarled in annoyance at my eavesdropping. With that, I retreated quickly and continued on my way.

Deciding to take a shortcut, I crossed an old farm field now covered with tall grass, milkweeds, and briar patches. While stopping to remove some of the prickly briars from my shirt sleeve, something could be heard shuffling in the grass just ahead of me. Letting my curiosity take over, I ignored the remaining burrs dangling from my shirt and angled toward this distraction. After just a few steps forward, I abruptly stopped and started backtracking. Fortunately, the black and white stripes before me, did not respond as I had feared. Avoiding what could have been a stinky situation, I began putting as much distance as I could between myself and this startled skunk.

When I was somewhat younger, I had this notion about getting a pet skunk. After reading an enticing ad in an *Outdoor Life* magazine, it convinced me that owning a de-scented skunk would be really cool. Even nowadays, I've often thought about what a great prank could be pulled on Boone with one of these notorious critters as a pet. However, the one now at hand represented the real deal and thus the need for a fast exit on my part.

Weaving through several sumac groves, I re-entered back into the woods. Looking back over my shoulder, I double-checked several times to make sure that skunk did not follow me. While trudging up the hillside to Sage's new home in the mine shaft. I saw his blue jay friend Snitch fluttering about. This of course meant that Sage had already been advised of my presence. Therefore, I sort of expected to see this owl waiting for me outside the mine's entrance. Instead, in the shadows of the birches was a strange looking figure sitting on the forest floor and resting with his back against several rocks. His dark eyes never blinked as he intently studied me. For what seemed like a long, long time, we just stared at each other.

While straining to asses this character, I could see that he had a dark complexion and long hair twisted into braids. The tints of gray upon his scalp foretold that he was of many years. At the back of his head was a single feather. Wearing no shirt, a medallion and chain dangled on his bare chest. Large metal spheres were attached to his ears. What struck me most, was the shape of this figure. As he began to stand up, I became startled by his stature. Although appearing to be quite old, this man was no taller than a fourth grade child. His body seemed quite pudgy in nature and disproportionate to his height. All the tales previously told to me now flashed in my mind. Without hesitation, I knew exactly who stood facing me. This was indeed the Elf Indian!

Before either of us said anything, the silence was broken by a voice from behind me. "I see that you have met Tustis," said Sage. Responding to my owl friend, I replied, "Not exactly." Turning toward Tustis, I then

nervously asked, "Are you the Elf Indian?" Caught in thought, Tustis waited momentarily and then answered, "I have been referred to as many things including elf Indian, red dwarf, pygmy, half-pint, pipsqueak, midget, imp, and shorty. I prefer to be called Tustis."

Somehow, I felt as if this extraordinary man may have been insulted by the reference of elf. I apologized and noted that the elf term instinctively came from so many of the stories I had heard about him. Again, caught up in thought, Tustis paused and then responded by instructing me to sit and listen carefully to the story of his family legacy. Tustis began by explaining that he is a shaman and that his name means "weaver of dreams". Due to this distinction, he carefully studies all visions which come to him. In a recent series of recurring visions, a "leaning boy" appears each time. With his eyes sternly focused on me Tustis then proclaimed, "And now, that boy sits before me."

Although my stature had always been one of tilting to the side, never had I considered myself as a leaning person. Taken aback, I was not sure if this represented another label being tagged on me. However, I had just referred to this Indian man as an elf, and therefore needed to temper my own feelings about his reference to me. Nonetheless, the serious look now stenciled on Tustis's face gave me an uneasy feeling of suddenly being chosen for some kind of ritual.

Because of the ongoing revelations which come to him, Tustis deemed it important for me to know of his shaman practices and tribal heritage. As he continued on, Tustis described his role within the Clan of the Owl. Unique to his family, every other generation produces a small man like himself. In his culture, this difference is revered. As such, he became distinguished as a healer and prophet, like that of his grandfather, Talon. Tustis then told me that the local stories, I have heard, refer more so to his grandfather than himself.

As a shaman, Tustis shared that he is prone to visions of things to come. Yesterday, in his most recent vision, he foresaw a leaning boy, small Indian, robed man, old woman, and an owl, all gathered together in a council circle. To clarify this vision, he needed to consult the dream pool. Seeing that I was confused by his reference to a dream pool, Tustis then began explaining to me what this meant. He noted that not far from this spot is a trickling waterfall at the end of a narrow canyon. Well hidden, very few know that this waterfall even exists. As the water cascades over the rocks above, it forms a small pool below. According to Tustis, this is a dream pool. By lying in this pool, Tustis's visions are washed into the water and reflected back. Upon stepping out of this pool and studying the picture it reveals, Tustis is able to more clearly understand his visions.

Prior to our encounter this morning, Tustis visited the dream pool to study his vision of myself and the others. Through the pool's reflection, it became clear that I held a book that must somehow be connected to everyone in the council circle. However, the pool's reflection could not say how this book came to be or what it contained.

As Tustis spoke, he had an aura about him. His wisdom and sincerity were beyond any doubt. Because the things he now talked of, sounded so magical and mysterious, I found myself entranced by his words. Although I had never before been referred to as "the leaning boy", this description of me did make sense. However, trying to understand my kinship to this Shaman's vision left me more than baffled.

I definitely knew of this waterfall to which Tustis referred. It is indeed hidden and not known to many others. As a waterway, it is neither massive nor magnificent. Created by a tiny spring beginning near my home, this descending water eventually flows over a four-story high bluff, forms a small pool, and then winds its way to form a nearby lake in Cox Hollow. From there, it drains to another lake in Twin Valley. Below the earthen dam of this second lake, the flowing water gains the title of Mill Creek as it meanders past the old Hyde sawmill and numerous cow pastures. After many twists and turns, this stream empties into a huge river named after this state. Finally, what begins as just droplets continues westward to merge with the Big Muddy. What an incredible journey from just a tiny dream pool to a mighty river of dreams.

Depending on the season, this discrete waterfall can be a considerable flowage following the spring thaw or summer deluges. By the start of autumn, there is little more than just a trickle. In wintertime, this watery cascade comes to a complete standstill as huge icicles form from top to bottom. Sheltered by rock walls and a canopy of trees, this mossy and fern-laden place serves as a forest refuge during heat waves. These same rock walls bounce eerie echoes from one side to the other. Most of all, this is the special hideout where I found my first arrowheads.

Learning about the dream pool was something I never heard of before. I could not imagine lying in its icy cold water for any length of time. However, my ability to understand new things had now become enhanced due to a small wonder Indian and an earth owl.

As Tustis paused in his storytelling and I sat thinking about the dream pool, Sage interrupted this intermission by saying, "Tustis, perhaps you need to speak also of the mine symbols." Tustis again paused for a moment of contemplation and then responded by telling me, that at first sunlight on this morning, he viewed the three markings on the wall of the lead ore mine. Tustis stated these markings were familiar within his tribe. The face drawing portrayed the owl symbol of his family clan. The animal track warned of the "wildering beast", which Tustis said could be that of a ram, bull, stag, boar, or any split hoofed creature which has lost its way.

When it came to the strangely contorted drawing, Tustis had more to say. The spooky silhouette was a figure known as an "Oakist". According to Tustis, for many years, a legend has been passed along by his people about the giants who once roamed this land. As these giants grew old and weary, they slowed down and took root into the earth, thus becoming misshapen trees called Oakists. Some Oakists are tall and willowy, while others may be stubby, stout, and grossly disfigured. Many are barren of leaves, busted with broken branches, and have begun to hollow. Each stands out as a haggard-looking misfit within the forest. Tustis noted that Oakists can also be found as lone trees in farm fields. While the earth changes around them, these sacred sentries remained untouched. Any person of honor and good heart, who sits beneath the branches of an Oakist, is granted some of the wisdom shared by this tree. Anyone daring to cut down or destroy an Oakist, would as a consequence, endure a lifetime of bad luck. After hearing all this, I asked Tustis if there were Oakists in these woods. He responded that indeed there were and that I had most likely encountered at least one. He then assured me that Sage's former home was not an Oakist, and therefore, no ill will would befall me.

Looking to his right at the mine shaft opening, the old Shaman seemed lost in thought. Appearing perplexed, Tustis finally turned to me and said that it was a mystery to him as to who had painted the three symbols. He also wondered why these paintings came to be here in this makeshift tunnel. Tustis then explained that the combination of these markings foretold a prophecy. "Perhaps," Tustis remarked, "I will soon need to climb Percussion Rock and seek this answer within another vision."

Having heard tales about Percussion Rock, I had yet to see this storied structure. Located near a rugged area named Hunter's Hollow, it is several miles north of my home and part of what folks around here call Wyoming Valley. Grandpa Nutter told me that Percussion Rock is a sacred place to the First Nation peoples of this region. Ceremonies were once performed atop this rock until the early settlers drove out most of the local Native Americans. Because of what Grandpa Nutter has told me, I asked Tustis if he could share more with me about this special place.

Tustis confirmed that Percussion Rock is indeed a sacred site and now visited solely by him, because his tribal people are long gone from this area. As such, he is the lone guardian of all souls linked to this spiritual rock. Tustis then noted that Percussion Rock was not the only sacred site in this area. Not far from where we currently sat, is a huge jutting bluff named Eenie Point. It has become a well-known landmark and one of the park's major tourist attractions. The main park road through Cox Hollow twists around this inspiring stony outcropping. Looking somewhat somber, Tustis told me that this particular bluff was a "Coming of Age Rock" to members of his clan. As a sign of entering into manhood, young Indian boys would climb this rock and perform a ritual known as the owl dance. Dressed in an elaborate feathered outfit, a routine of chants and movements would continue until the dancer was completely exhausted. Now unable to keep from smiling, Tustis recalled his youthful time of performing this lost ritual of the past. He also recollected the figure of an owl dancer that appeared years ago on the face of this stony formation. It was painted by an artist friend of his grandfather. Although now weathered away, faded traces of this painting can still be seen when the lighting is just right.

Tustis also noted that in the clearing which lies between Eenie Point and the dream pool stream, many traditional powwows were held. Lasting for several days, they involved dancing, pageantry, games, and a huge feast.

In the autumn of last year, I ventured down to Eenie Point and climbed to the top of this rock. The narrow ledges and steep grade make this a treacherous trek. Lined with pine needles, this steep trail can send you slipping and sliding at any time. Giant crevices abound everywhere. Protruding gnarly roots of age-old conifers bulge out from these openings. Like twisted sinister appendages, it almost seems as if these

roots are poised to reach out and grab anyone nearby. Topping off the plateau of Eenie Point is an enormous fissure. This jagged gap appears bent on swallowing up those who dare to straddle it. While cresting Eenie Point, it often feels as if the wind is being conjured into thrusting you upon the adjacent tree tops. Incredibly panoramic with its view of the valley below, this special place seems both spiritual and haunting.

According to Tustis, another important bluff nearby, yet outside of the park, also represented sacred ancestral grounds to his clan. They called it Deer Shelter Rock. Although he often travelled to this bluff for meditation, Tustis claimed that it was no longer possible to go there, because this site was now being developed into some kind of house on the rock. Looking again somber, Tustis cast his eyes downward and said, "As each day passes, another part of First Nation heritage becomes lost to what others call progress."

After relating so much about his people and this area, Tustis announced to me that he must now leave, yet would share more with me at a later time. With that, he quickly walked off and disappeared into the forest. According to Sage, this abrupt departure was common for Tustis. As a nomadic loner, this small wonder of an Indian always seemed shy about spending any length of time in one place.

In the weeks that followed, I saw Tustis again several times, during which, we exchanged many stories about ourselves. On one particular outing, Tustis led me down to Cox Hollow Lake and explained that before the dam was built to flood this basin, the area had been a meeting place for local tribes. I then shared with Tustis that this lake represented the place where my dad first took me fishing. Although dad and I had anticipated catching all kinds of bass and bluegills, the only fish that got hooked and landed was a big fat bullhead. Putting a huge bend in my fishing rod, I thought it might pull me right into the lake. Dad then instructed me on how to carefully unhook this fish without getting stung. Some people think that it is a bullhead's or catfish's whiskers which do the stinging, yet it is nasty spines at the end of each side fin which painfully prick you.

Excited at this being my first ever catch, I insisted we take it home to show mom. Although dad initially hesitated at this notion, a sneaky sort of smile crossed his face as he agreed we would make this a real surprise for her. He then fetched a pail from his truck, had me fill it with water, and then dropped the foot long bullhead into it. Dad relished pranks and was about to commit one. After arriving home, we began to execute the plan which dad shared with me during the ride back. While dad distracted mom, I snuck through the kitchen to empty the pail and bullhead into the sink. Finally, with dad escorting mom into the kitchen, she smiled at me and said, "I understand you have something special to show me." In response, I pointed to the sink. Just as mom bent over to look closer, the bullhead began flopping about. Mom's face turned pale as she began screaming, "Get that horrible thing out of here!" Terrified and still screaming, mom then retreated across the room. While trying to control his laughter, dad exclaimed, "But its tonight's supper!" With a look of scorn on her face, mom then stared dad down and retorted, "There is no way I am going to cook or eat anything that ugly. Get it out of here right now." Realizing that he might have taken this prank a little too far, dad quickly retrieved the fish and took it over to our neighbor Reuben, a hardcore angler who fished for and ate just about anything that swam. As I finished this story, Tustis peered out at the lake and noted to me, "When I was a young boy and only a small stream flowed through this valley, my father brought me here to fish as well. Though our experiences vary, I find it quite good that each of us has a memorable connection to this place."

Just like Grandpa Nutter, Tustis was a remarkable storyteller. He shared with me tales about vision quests, brother wolf, white buffalo prophecies, coyote the trickster, and Bigfoot, whom Tustis referred to as the "Great Hairy Man". There were also spooky legends involving dancing skeletons and skin walkers. In a sadder refrain, Tustis recalled as well the sagas of his peoples being driven from these lands and the broken promises of treaties.

Although apprehensive about directly asking, I tried several times to find out about Tustis's tribal affiliation. "My people," Tustis would say, "are of many nations." Sometimes he would talk of the Oneida, which he referred to as the "People of the Rock." Other times, he mentioned the Winnebago and Ho-Chunk, calling them the "People near the Dirty Water." Most often however, it was the Sauk, Fox, Chippewa, and Sioux who became part of his tales. Showing great sadness, Tustis also noted to me that as a Clan of the Owl member, he was the lone survivor.

Being a shaman healer, Tustis took great interest in the nature of my legs. Showing sensitivity and concern, he wanted to know how this situation affected my well-being and self-perception. Like Sage, Tustis advised me not to be wrongly influenced by the bullying of others or to underestimate all that I could achieve. What impressed me most from Tutstis was a saying passed on to him from his grandfather, who said, "Those who are less than perfect are more than gifted." I think of these insightful words often, especially when I am struggling in a frustrating situation. With all that is being taught to me by both Tustis and Sage, it almost seems as if I am discovering a new inner strength while becoming an old wise owl as well. In other words and other ways, I am slowly but surely, learning to be okay as otherwise.

# THE CHURCH WINDOW

> *A book can indeed be judged by its cover, once you*
> *have looked inside and read between the lines.*

When a soldier comes home from war, the memories and injuries all too often return with him. According to Grandpa Nutter, that's exactly what happened to a local guy named Oliver Lucas. Just out of high school, Oliver enlisted into the U.S. Army and soon got shipped overseas. He landed in a foreign place which many of us had rarely heard of and knew little about. While most of his hometown buddies were hoping not to be drafted, Oliver eagerly signed on to serve. During his high school days, Oliver showed incredible promise as both an artist and musician. He was so good at playing piano that a full university scholarship had been offered to Oliver in his senior high school year.

As much as Oliver wanted to pursue his music and artwork, something interrupted his ambitions. Oliver's older brother had been drafted two years earlier and was now listed as missing in action. No one knew whether his brother had been killed or taken prisoner. He was Oliver's big brother and closest friend. Rather than going off to college, Oliver joined the Army in hopes of being deployed to Vietnam and finding his brother. In doing so, Oliver found out just how brutal and bitter war can be.

Two months into his tour of duty, Oliver's troop got ambushed. During the battle that ensued, a land mine exploded near Oliver and killed two of his buddies. The blast was so intense that it left Oliver completely deaf in one ear and very limited of hearing in the other. Shrapnel wounds also caused nerve damage to his left hand. Although Oliver and the rest of his troop managed to fight off the enemy, Oliver soon found himself being shipped back home. With his hearing gone, the war appeared over for this injured soldier.

Like many military veterans returning from battle, Oliver came back to a place where family and friends did not understand what he had gone through. Being a combat veteran and connected to what evolved into an unpopular war, made his situation even more difficult. It seemed as if both the politicians and protesters were allowing soldiers such as Oliver to be blamed for this war. No parades or appreciation existed for those serving their country at this time.

Recovering from the loss of his Army buddies and loss of hearing was tremendously hard for Oliver. He felt a sense of failure by getting injured and not finding his brother, who remained listed as missing in action. The forlorn piano in Oliver's family home became a constant reminder of what once was to be his future. Depressed and angry about his current life, Oliver attempted to drown his problems by drinking heavily. Many local residents came to fear him because of his boozed-up outbursts. Public intoxication caused Oliver to also have a number of run-ins with the local police. He regularly served as the subject for gossip on the telephone party lines. Some even branded him the official town drunk. As such, Oliver eventually diminished into a loner and outcast. When it seemed that this military veteran had sunk to his lowest point, Oliver suddenly disappeared. As months went by, many in this community feared that something tragic had happened to him. Efforts to locate Oliver continued without success. However, almost three years to the date when he disappeared, Oliver mysteriously resurfaced. Adding to this mystery was the brown hooded robe and sandals he now wore. Fulfilling a monk-like persona, Oliver moved into an abandoned country chapel, not far from Grandpa Nutter's. Although rarely seen venturing into town anymore, the locals started referring to him as Brother Oliver.

Taking up residence in an orphaned country church is not unique to this community. Just northeast of town, an isolated chapel near Evans Quarry got transformed into a hippie commune. Many area residents wonder just what goes on there, and yet, there are just as many local folks who do not want to know anything about the happenings at this place. Those occupying this church are referred to as longhairs, peaceniks, and flower children. From what Grandpa Nutter has told me, these hippies pretty much keep to themselves, and the rest of us, just keep away.

Sage had mentioned Brother Oliver's name to me several times and also described him as otherwise. In regards to Tustis's vision, he suggested that perhaps this monk was the robed figure. Although I had never personally met this man, the Old Rock Church he now dwelled within, was less than a mile from my home. With an ancient age, adjacent cemetery of weathered headstones, and off-the-beaten path location, the spiritual setting of this church had a spooky nature about it. While this country chapel lay empty for many years, local tales were often told of a chapel bell ringing and choirs singing in the middle of the night. Some even profess that the souls of the pilgrim farmers gather here monthly as a congregation. Claiming to be mystics and mediums, strange visitors occasionally trespass on this property. Combined with the fact that it is now occupied by a reclusive hooded hermit, the murky legacy of this sanctuary has kept me from venturing close by.

Grandpa told me that not only did his grandfather Christianson help to build the Old Rock Church, yet this ancestor of mine and many other relatives are buried in its cemetery. The closest I ever came to meandering near the Old Rock Church was during a visit to a neighboring farm. This farm belongs to a man who Grandpa calls, "George-of-all-trades". Mind you, this is not the same George with the in-town junkyard. According to Grandpa Nutter, this George is a trucker, excavator, woodcutter, snow plowman, landlord, contractor, saddle peddler, and most of all, a genuine horse trader. Grandpa noted that not only is George a horseman, but also a collector of horse drawn things including an authentic stagecoach, vintage buckboards, winter cutters, and an old surrey with fringe on the top. Hidden away in area barns and warehouses, this guy had enough stuff to form his own wagon train.

Although referred to as a farm, George's property is really more like a rodeo ranch. Because George is grooming his three sons Jim, Terry, and Tom to compete in rodeos, his wild west-like place has its own corral and training arena. What's really intriguing as well is that wrangler George owns a massive and menacing rodeo bull named Caesar. Along with his cowboy hat, faded blue jeans, and scuffed boots, George had one distinguishing feature which led to some calling him the "Big O". Wrapped around his waistline was a broad leather-tooled belt with an enormous silver buckle spelling out the word "GEORGE". Due to his many years of bouncing around either on horseback or in diesel cabs, all the letters accept the "O", broke loose and broke off. With this one letter left prominently exposed, the "Big O" nickname took root.

In regards to the nearby park, perhaps no one knows this area better than George. Because of the huge horse herd he maintains, sometimes numbering over one hundred head, George organizes saddleback rides into the park and has blazed many of its trails. Outside this park, George has also become influential in organizing area Boots & Saddle Clubs, which are somewhat like rural YMCA's for horse riders. As an excavator, George also demolished, dismantled, and even moved many of the original farmstead buildings which once dotted this park.

At this stage in my young impressionable life, I had become infatuated with anything having to do with range-riding cowboys, gunslingers, and American Indians. This phase began a few years back when cereal companies started promoting Wild West posters on the back of their boxes. In order to get the complete series of outlaws and Indian chiefs, I gobbled up all the Sugar Smacks and Sugar Pops possible. Mailing in the box tops from some other cereals, I also attained a neat replica of Fort Apache. To acquire a collection of Roy Rodgers comic books, my marble set of peeries, plunkers, and cat eyes got traded. A grade school lunchbox of mine showed off Hopalong Cassidy. Target shooting with a lever-action Daisy Model 94 BB gun, established me as a backyard bounty hunter. On my bedroom dresser is the genuine miniature totem pole I bought while visiting Wisconsin Dells. One of these days, I might even dare to wear that beaded Indian belt purchased there as well.

Every chance available, my attention focuses toward the popular television westerns playing on Grandpa's black and white Zenith. Similar to most kids in this era, I long to be a rowdy wrangler in *Rawhide*, bad-guy-scaring character like Marshall Matt Dillon in *Gunsmoke*, or a brother to Hoss, Adam, and Little Joe in *Bonanza*. Being able to shoot a ring-levered gun like Lucas McCain in *The Rifleman*, would be really cool. Riding a buckboard through hostile territories in *Wagon Train* seems cool as well. Proving to be a formidable gunslinger, I'd love to flash Paladin's *Have Gun-Will Travel* card. Sometimes I dream of owning a fringed buckskin coat like that of *Cheyenne*. If I could just get a white horse, white hat, black mask, and a pair of pearl-handled six-shooters, I could be another galloping hero resembling *The Lone Ranger*. I'd cherish being a Tonto sidekick as well. Fascinated with the characters in these TV shows, I viewed George as the closest thing to a real-life cowboy in this neck of the woods.

The only thing bad about my current addiction to TV westerns is getting one of the theme songs stuck in my teenage head. While daydreaming in the classroom, I often keep hearing the Rollin' Rollin' Rollin' tune from *Rawhide*. It seems to be the main one echoing over and over in my mind. This is partly due to the fact that a *Rawhide* buckaroo character called Rowdy Yates has become my favorite. He is played by a young actor named Clint Eastwood, whom I think might someday get to be really famous.

If all this six-shooter and saddlebag talk about wranglers, rustlers, and cowpokes makes me appear to be drifting off on a tangent, without a doubt, this deviation is deliberate. Not all my time is spent rabblerousing through the nearby woodsy park and hanging out with its motley crew. Just like most kids of my age, I spend far too much time watching the boob tube, anxiously yearning to become a big star, and dreaming of new horizons. Right now, my focus is toward the Wild West and my curious cowboy neighbor "Big O" George. And as for horseman George living right next door to the Old Rock Church, I definitely suspect that he could tell me more than anyone else, about the mysterious Brother Oliver.

Until now, the only wild-west experiences of my youth involve a place in town which everyone calls Harry's horse barn. Located on the property where Crystal Lake once flourished, Harry maintains a stable where locals board their horses. Even though Harry pretends to be a gruff and cantankerous old caretaker, he allows area kids to routinely ride his ponies on a first come, first serve basis. While still living in town, I got to trot, canter, and gallop along Harry's trails, which crisscross through old ore digs and mine tailings. At the far end of these trails is a dilapidated shack inhabited by the notorious Bushkee sisters. These quirky spinsters serve as the subjects of many local Spine-tingling legends. Often they are viewed like bewitching characters out of a Grimm's fairy tale. Based on what my friends and I were told by the older kids, we dare not venture anywhere close to these spooky ladies. One guy even tried to tell me that if captured by the Busjkees, they would roast you in the slag furnace, a nearby chimney structure leftover from the mining era. Nowadays, I have even thought about the prospect of convincing these sinister sisters to kidnap Boone.

Now that I have become older and moved out to Grandpa's home, riding around on little parade ponies no longer seems as thrilling. To be a real wrangler, one needs to hang around real horses. On most days out here in the country, I usually hear horse whinnying sounds echoing from George's farm. Like a lot of wannabe cowpokes, I am fascinated with horses, especially based on some of the stories Grandpa told me about these hay burners. As a history buff, Grandpa always had to instruct me on the origin of things. He said that when Spaniards first introduced horses to this country, the Native Americans had no word for these particular animals, and therefore, began referring to them as "Elk Dogs". Being as big as the familiar elk and able to carry burdens like dogs, they viewed horses as a combination of these two critters. Grandpa then went on to educate me that the Native American word for elk was wapiti, which translates as "white rump". My grandfather seems to have a knack in coming up with this weird kind of Indian stuff. Grandpa's knowledge of Native Americans often makes me wonder as to what connection he actually has with this culture.

When it comes to talking about horses, Grandpa Nutter also likes to proclaim that a notorious local ghost, known as the Ridgeway Phantom, often appears as a black stallion. Many of the farmers, who once lived east of town, experienced seeing this four-legged specter as it roamed about in their fields. Grandpa even speculates that this ghost might be a fabled Irish Kelpie. Stories about Kelpies are by far the creepiest of which my grandfather tells. The mythical Kelpie is a devil spirit which disguises itself as an ebony horse. Its' hide is like that of a seal and cold as death to the touch. Kelpies entice wanderers to climb atop them for a ride. Once accomplished, this horse gallops off, hell-bent for the nearest lake or river. Upon arriving, it tosses the rider into the water and attempts to drown him.

While tracing family roots, Grandpa would oftentimes sadly recall the loss of his maternal grandfather, due to what he called a demon horse. As the village blacksmith, his grandfather died after being kicked in the chest while shoeing this wicked draft horse. Grandpa also blamed the death of another relative on unruly horses which spooked and tipped over a logging wagon. His stories often told of tragedies like these, which Grandpa Nutter noted were all too commonplace among the early settlers. He reminded me as well, how an ornery farm horse had once bitten my mother on the shoulder and left ugly teeth marks, which lasted for months. To further emphasize his point about horses being nasty, Grandpa said they were about the only critters that actually eat the thistle giants.

Unlike Grandpa Nutter, I did not consider horses as bad news beasts and instead, had a great curiosity about them. I also knew just where to find these animals. After hearing about all the things going on at George's, I decided on this day to get my silver Schwinn out of grandpa's tool shed and rustle on down the road to this intriguing place. It had been quite some time since the bike was last ridden. While living in town, I raced up and down the side streets and sometimes explored the alleys in between. Using clothespins to attach baseball cards to the bike's frame, a motorized sound got created as they flipped through the wheel spokes. It was just one of those dumb kid things you do while pretending to be riding a motorcycle. This bicycle also once had a big goofy horn mounted on the handlebars. Now absent of the cards and horn, this bike could again be ridden with its dignity restored.

While climbing aboard this two-wheeler, I began flashing back to one of my first biking adventures. Although reluctant at first, some of the neighborhood kids let me tag along one day on a ride to Brennan's Bridge. Located on the outskirts of town, trekking to this destination became a rite of passage for local kids. It involved traveling down Division Street, peddling quickly past the East Side Cemetery and the Bushkees' house, and then finally turning onto County Highway 191, for a one and a half mile glide to Brennan's Bridge. Once reached, the next hour or so would be spent fishing, throwing rocks in the water, or just balancing on the bridge rails. To most, this bridge was nothing more than an ordinary road crossing a small creek. For young adventurers, it served as a distinguished destination.

Toward the opposite outskirts and heading west from town, lies another rite of passage location dubbed "The Culvert". Though unspectacular like Brennan's Bridge, it is nonetheless, another Neverland escape from all adults. For those of us who explored about on wire-spoke wheels, these journeys simply represented an expansion of boundaries. Of course, now that I have matured way beyond this kind of escapade, bigger and better adventures awaited me.

Cautiously peddling away, I just had to see for myself all the horsing around at George's. As in the past, the bike's fenders and chain guard began rattling. No matter how often I tighten them, they always worked loose. This was now prompted even more so by riding along the bumpy gravel shoulder of the highway. By no means could I sneak up on anyone with this noisy contraption. Nonetheless, the freedom of being on the open road made this trek worthwhile. And in just a few minutes, my destination would be reached.

Usually I avoided riding my bike for two very good reasons. First of all, my oddball legs caused me to cruise about in an off kilter manner. My shorter leg had to stretch as far as possible in order to reach the right peddle. On the left side, my longer leg seemed always cramped and could never extend fully. Although always uncomfortable, this two-wheeler transported me to destinations both near and far. That is the reason my dad continually encouraged me to ride. However, my bike was the last Christmas present ever given to me by dad, and for this reason, this bike is a sad reminder of someone I miss so much. Perhaps wheeling over to George's would help fulfill some the adventures that dad had always wished for me. With that in mind, I bobbled along and peddled onward with a "Hi-Yo Silver".

While drawing closer to where the high-fenced practice arena was located, I caught a glimpse of several people riding about and practicing turns with their horses. Having been so dry lately, the area within the arena resembled a dust storm in progress. While wiping some of this dust from my eyes and peering through the openings between the fence boards, my movements caught the eye of a middle-aged man in a wide brimmed cowboy hat. Before having any time to react, I nervously stared as this rider and his horse headed rapidly toward me. Not sure as to whether I would now be in trouble for spying, my legs began preparing to jump down from the fence and run. Instead however, my reaction became that common to most scared kids. I simply froze in place. Upon climbing down from his horse and turning to face me, a stinging sunbeam suddenly poked me in the eyes. This ray of light reflected off a huge belt buckle with just an "O" in the middle. No longer did any doubt exist in my mind, about who this was. As my hands held firm to the fence rail, this man looked at me and said, "You must be that kid from just down the road at Nutter's house." In sheepish response I answered, "Yes, Grandpa Nutter is my Grandpa." After saying so, I then realized how dumb this sounded. "Well then," answered the man, "I'm George and I'll bet your granddad has told you all kinds of stories about me." Not wanting to get Grandpa Nutter in any kind of trouble for gossiping, I replied, "No, not really. All I know is that Grandpa refers to you as George-of-all-trades."

Laughing at what I had just noted, George then remarked, "There's no better storyteller than your grandfather and I'd have to agree with that title he's given me."

After tying the reins of his horse to the nearby rail, George studied me for a few seconds and then inquired, "Have you ever ridden a horse before?" "Only the ponies down at Harry's horse barn," I replied. Relating to what I had just said, George grinned and responded, "That's where most wranglers around here get their start. Perhaps now, you might like to try something more man-sized like that pinto over there."

Looking across the corral to another fenced in area, I could see the black and white horse George had pointed to. It reminded me of Scout, the Pinto ridden by Tonto. Little Joe rode the same kind at the Ponderosa. It was not a particularly large horse and had sort of a friendly look to it. Putting on a front and attempting to appear old enough to do so, I quickly fired back, "Sure, I can do that." George then replied, "If you think that Nutter won't mind, I'll saddle her up. Without having any time to reconsider this whole ordeal, I soon found myself helped up into the saddle and straddled atop this horse. Being a cowboy fanatic and now sitting tall in the saddle, this was a dream come true.

Although I had at first felt somewhat self-conscious about my uneven legs, this became no concern for George as he adjusted the stirrups on each side. As George began instructing me about neck reining, balancing in the saddle, and controlling the horse, everything happening at this point now seemed to be spinning around in my head. These motions then moved on to the rest of my body as this spotted horse began trotting forward. As the spirited bronco maneuvered around the arena, its speed increased. Before I knew what to do, my accelerating ride had now escalated into a full speed gallop. Out of control and inexperienced, I did not have a clue as what to do. With my right hand, I held onto the leather reins, while the left hand latched tightly onto the saddle horn. Using leg muscles that I did not know even existed, I squeezed the horse's ribs as hard as possible. Charging forward and moving hell bent, it seemed this mustang had made up its mind to charge toward the barn at the east end of this riding area. With the wooden doors wide open to this building, it now became evident to me that my steed had every intention of storming into it. Hanging on for life, I did the only thing I could to save myself. I ducked under the upper door frame just as the horse ran into this building. With this rampaging hay-burner in total command of the next move, it then came to an abrupt stop and thus avoided crashing through the far end. An excited George came running up to me, stopped for a moment to catch his breath, and then exclaimed, "Holy buckets! I am sure glad you've got your head still intact." Sensing that I was somewhat shocked by this experience, George then tried to lighten the mood by saying, "Never have I seen anybody hold on and ride like that. Maybe you should try the bull next!"

Embarrassed by what had happened, I never told Grandpa Nutter nor any of my friends about this haphazard escapade. However, while meandering around George's place after this hair-raising event, I did catch a good look at the Old Rock Church and cemetery just behind his place. As such, I continued being curious about the lone man living there. Compared to the rambling ride I had just experienced, nothing else, including a strange monk, seemed quite as scary anymore.

Grandpa Nutter told me that many of the locals consider Brother Oliver as a screwball. Some of the God-faring gossips claim it is blasphemy that he dresses in such a holy manner. Few bothered to talk about the sacrifices made by this wounded warrior. My grandfather, who had also fought in a war, said that Brother Oliver was being judged too harshly and deserved more respect than scrutiny. He saw no reason for anyone to fear or forsake this soldier. Grandpa also said that there was far more to Brother Oliver than most realize. In short order, I would learn just that.

Ten days had passed since my rambunctious horse ride. As the dawn brought sunlight into the bedroom, my awakening thoughts focused on this morning's impending trek. Today, I would now have the chance to form my own opinion of Brother Oliver. Just the week before, Sage had instructed me that for our next rendezvous, a meeting had been arranged with the mysterious monk. Complicating matters this morning was a slight stomach ache which I earned from the night before. As a result of this minor medical issue, I got a late start. Now heading off into the woods, I felt nervous and uneasy. While approaching Sage's hillside home, I could see his huge yellow eyes watching me. With his feathers ruffled a bit, he seemed nervous as well. "You're late", scolded Sage. "I have been waiting here for quite some time."

Noting Sage's disappointment, an explanation seemed needed. "Because of last night," I explained, "it was hard getting out of bed this morning. Being this is Dairy month, the bank in town gives out free chocolate milk every Friday night. As such, my friends and I meet there to see who can drink the most cups. Though I did not drink anywhere near to the twenty-plus cups that my friend Harley chugged down, my stomach reminded me this morning, of what had taken place yesterday. Sage then just looked at me and remarked, "You humans do the craziest things." Trying to redeem myself, I responded back, "Well, the chocolate milk stand is also a good place to meet cute 4-H farm girls." Nodding in approval, Sage then uttered, "Now that part makes a little more sense. However, because I finally remembered something really important, we have no time to lose and must hurry along." With this marching order, both of us set ourselves in motion. While doing so, Sage began babbling about the owl symbol in his new home. Although this marking on the mine wall seemed familiar to him, Sage could not recall where he had seen it before. Now however, he once again remembered. Several years ago, when Sage first met Brother Oliver, this monk showed him a dream catcher. Centered on the leather patch of this special piece, was the same owl symbol. Both excited and curious, Sage needed to know the connection between the dream catcher owned by Brother Oliver and the drawing on the old mine wall.

Although Grandpa Nutter had mentioned something about a dream catcher in one of his stories, whatever these things were remained unfamiliar to me. Therefore, I needed to call upon Sage's wisdom and ask him just what dream catchers were. After replying, "They are part me and part First Nation heritage," Sage gave me a lengthy lecture about these handcrafted items. For many generations, dream catchers have been revered within First Nation culture and traditions. Signifying strength and unity, this creation begins as a rawhide or bent wood hoop. Added to the circular form is a crisscrossing web of leather strips and dangling feathers. Sometimes brightly colored beads are included as well.

Native Americans believe that the night air is filled with dreams, both good and bad. The dream catcher, when hung over or near a sleeping person and swinging freely in the air, catches the dreams as they flow by. The good dreams know how to pass through the dream catcher, slipping through the outer holes and sliding down the feathers to the sleeper. The bad dreams get tangled in the dream catcher's webbing and perish with the first light of the new day. Nowadays, many folks have forgotten their true meaning and wrongly interpret dream catchers as decorative works of art or lucky charms sold in souvenir shops. Cocking his head back in a show of pride, Sage proclaimed, "Many of the dream catchers created by Tustis showcase some of the feathers which I have shed. In fact, Tustis and I first met during his ongoing searches for feathers"

With this lesson on dream catchers completed, our journey again resumed. Leading the way, Sage noted to me that we would be venturing to an area known as the "Church Window". It represented a whimsical canopy of trees shaped like a cathedral arch. Although this thing called the Church Window was unknown to me, I was more than well aware of strange tree formations. Hereabouts in these woods, the trees themselves are critters. Their personalities and statures vary immensely. While some trees reach toward the sky and attempt to snag the clouds, others just hunch over as if wearied by so many seasons. Though their movements are oftentimes too slow to readily perceive, it is evident that they stretch out in all directions, lean sideways, sway a bit, and even topple at old age.

As for being rooted critters, some of these trees are downright scary. For example, there is an ominous section I refer to as the "Dead Woods". Within it are all kinds of zombie trees. Twisted and tilted, these timbers are creepy and haunting. Though now deceased, these trees somehow seem as if they could come back to life and terrify everything around them. Some even appear to be attacking each other. Grandpa Nutter told me that this area had once been struck by a fierce lightning storm. On the darkest of nights, he claims that these dead trees ever so slightly glow in the dark.

Other trees within these woods have become storied landmarks as well. On one of the ridges where so many mushrooms grow, is the fattest tree in this forest. Sage refers to it as the raggedy oak. Stemming from the enormous rotund trunk of this acorn-bearing behemoth, its branches toss and turn in every direction. Many are battered and busted by nature's fury. This spooky-looking tree is grounded by protruding roots that reach out and seem to be clawing the earth. Come autumn, its jagged leaves become copper in color. Among all the trees in this area, it is always the last to lose its leaves in the fall. According to Sage, this magical tree of sorts is a forest guardian. Since being told the story of the enchanted Oaksts by Tustis, I often now wonder as to whether this particular tree is indeed one of these mythical giants.

On the ridge where the hidden waterfall begins its descent to the dream pool, there is an apple orchard of heirloom trees. Planted years ago by the first European settlers in this region, this fruity grove has been long abandoned and is now only harvested by critters such as the whitetail deer, which rise up on their hind legs and pluck apples from the gnarled

lower branches. Although these apples are usually quite small, misshapen, and pock-marked, I have never tasted a better apple during the autumn ripening season. Also within this edible landscape are several groves of walnut and butternut, which like the apple trees attract a fair number of foraging critters. In past years, far too many of these trees also attracted woodcutters, who prized them for the crafting of furniture, gunstocks, and other woodworks. A lot of the current walnut saplings strewn throughout the hillsides are those planted by Grandpa Nutter. Helping these trees to make a comeback has always been his legacy.

Perhaps my most favorite tree is the one I have dubbed "Bear in the Hollow." Like the raggedy oak, its wide-angle trunk is enormous. However, this age-old tree is distinguished by an incredible hollow cavity, which at a distance, resembles the silhouette of a hefty black bear. This opening is so large that I can easily crawl into it and hide. As a mystical looking timber, you can envision an elf, troll, or even an actual bear, residing within it.

Just as magical, yet less intimidating, are the stately white pines that station themselves atop the jutting bluffs. Sometimes I visit these trees just to lounge in the bed of pine needles that have piled up beneath them. Listening carefully, you can definitely hear these conifers whispering. While doing so, I can also take in the strong pine scents associated with these lofty timbers. And if I should doze off while daydreaming under these trees, the nearby descent of a pine cone bombardment is sure to awaken me.

Not wanting to be remiss, I need to mention as well the ivory birch groves, which stand in such stark contrast to the rest of these woods. Huddled closely together, there always seems to be at least one or two fallen members, exposing the short lifespan of this spindly family. Each autumn, these whitewashed trees bestow onto the forest floor a carpet of golden leaves. By doing so, they transform area trails into Oz-like yellow brick roads. Fortunately, there are no lions, tigers, and bears along the way.

Despite so many resident trees becoming familiar landmarks to me, I had yet to discover each and every one of them in this forest. Soon I would make a new acquaintance. As Sage and I finally came within view of the Church Window, it was easily seen how this grove got its name. A line of trees bowed toward each other to create a chapel image. Walking into this wonder, I caught sight of a robed man who appeared to be meditating. He sat silently with legs crossed and head bent downward. His hands were folded tightly against his chest. Looking at Sage, I then whispered, "Maybe we should not interrupt him." Sage then answered back, He is expecting us and I have a way of letting him know we are coming." With that, Sage began beating his wings against his body. Even though he had great difficulty raising his bum wing, the intense flapping sounded off like a drumbeat. "This is something I learned from my grouse friends," said Sage. "And even though Brother Oliver cannot hear this sound, he feels the vibrations."

As usual, Sage was right. Brother Oliver lowered his arms and turned immediately toward us. Lifting his right hand, he signaled that we should continue forward. Upon getting closer to Brother Oliver, I could see that he was a tall man with a bushy dark beard. Deeply entrenched Crows' feet sprouted from the outside corners of his inquisitive eyes. Several small scars appeared on the left side of his face. Based on the stories told to me, I assumed these were remnants of war wounds.

What surprised me most about Brother Oliver involved the appearance of his age. From what I knew about him, he had to be somewhere in his mid-20's. Perhaps it was the beard, receding hairline, and drab attire which created a guise of being much older. The hooded brown robe covering this guy from head to toes was noticeably faded. His scuffed leather sandals exhibited considerable toil and travel. Standing so near to this notorious character, I could study every outward feature about him. However, nothing relating to this reclusive man seemed fearsome to me. Even before Brother Oliver began talking, I sensed a gentle nature about him. Nonetheless, this encounter made me nervous. Never before had I met or tried communicating with a deaf person.

Pausing momentarily and drawing a deep breath, Brother Oliver then noted in a soft-spoken voice, "I understand that we are all part of a Tustis vision. And from what I know of my shaman friend, his visions must be taken seriously." This robed man then turned directly to me and said. "Perhaps I should first introduce myself. I am known as Brother Oliver and perhaps you have heard many curious stories about me. Should you now have any questions for me, you can write them down on one of these pages." With that, Brother Oliver handed me a huge tablet of many pages. "It is my sketch pad, yet you can write in it as well." he said. As I grabbed hold of this book, it opened up and revealed a sketch of the woods. Seeing that I was studying this drawing, Brother Oliver remarked, "That's just something I started working on this morning. Go ahead and turn to one of the next blank pages."

Unsure of what to ask, I simply began writing down the first thing that came to my mine. At the top of the blank page I wrote, "Are you really a monk?" After giving me a skeptical look, Brother Oliver then replied, "Although not staying quite long enough to be ordained, I spent almost three years at a monastery, sobered up through some spiritual healing, and studied to be a monk. For the most part, I still continue this practice right here."

Scribbling again on the page I asked" Are you an artist as well?" Now taking on what appeared to be a smile of pride, Brother Oliver answered,

"My artwork is both my passion and healing." This question of his artistry vocation seemed to be the cue for something which Brother Oliver loved to talk about. After instructing Sage and I to sit down, Brother Oliver began sharing about how Sage had first brought him and Tustis together at this spot. As a healer, Tustis taught Brother Oliver that by coming to the Church Window and meditating, many of his war experiences could be overcome. When Tustis learned of Brother Oliver's artistic past, this shaman friend advised him that art could become part of his healing as well. Therefore, Brother Oliver noted that he now comes to this haven to study and sketch the woods around him. And what he sketches most often are Sage and the other critters who reside here.

Hearing this story from Brother Oliver, I had to ask him about a mysterious local artist whose owl sketches secretly appear in town. During the past couple of years, someone unseen has dropped off owl portraits at the local American Legion Hall. At the bottom of each artwork is the word "OWL" in capital letters. Attached each time is a note saying that this drawing should be auctioned off to help disabled veterans. That is exactly what the American Legion members do annually. Because these drawings have become so popular, thousands of dollars have been raised for veterans.

Scribbling away once again, I asked, "Do you know anything about the owl artist who helps veterans?" Brother Oliver hesitated a moment, smirked a bit, and then answered, "Yes, I know of him." Before giving me a chance for further inquiry, Sage interrupted and stated that I should ask Brother Oliver about his dream catcher and its symbol.

Once again I began jotting in this book. "Sage and I recently discovered a drawing in an old mine shaft that resembles the owl symbol on your dream catcher. Can you tell us about it?" Hesitating for a second time, Brother Oliver seemed caught up in thought before responding. He then replied that the dream catcher had belonged to the grandfather of his grandfather, a past relative whom family members seemed reluctant to talk about. Therefore, Brother Oliver confessed that he knew very little about this ancestor named William and could only assume that the dream catcher had once been a gift to his relative by its maker. As a very young boy, Brother Oliver's father gave him the dream catcher as a family heirloom, asked him to safeguard it, and yet, offered no explanation about this piece of Indian artwork, except to say that someday its mysterious meaning would be revealed. According to Brother Oliver, he is still waiting for that revelation.

Brother Oliver noted that many years ago he had taken this dream catcher to a Native American museum. The curator there told him this particular dream catcher was quite old and valuable. He also said that such a gift as this special piece would have only been given to someone being greatly honored.

When Brother Oliver's dream catcher first got viewed by Tustis, even this knowledgeable shaman could not explain the mystery surrounding it. Tustis however, recently told Brother Oliver that I may be the one to discover the answers. This notation of course, really confused and confounded me. Having come to the Church Window, I anticipated learning some new things. Instead, I now felt bewildered. According to the trio of Sage, Tustis, and Brother Oliver, I now represented some kind of role in solving a long time mystery about an age-old dream catcher and legendary owl symbol. As just a kid with so many questions, it did not make sense to me that I was the one with any answers.

Before departing from Brother Oliver, he insisted on telling me the story of how he first came to know this area of the woods. As a bashful and clumsy young boy, he often got picked on by local bullies, who one day talked him into coming out here for a snipe hunt. As the tradition goes, Brother Oliver was given a burlap bag and told to hide behind a big tree. In the meantime, the others in this group would go to the far side of the woods and chase the snipe toward him. As any snipe passed by, Brother Oliver was instructed to open up his bag and scoop up the feathered critter bearing a long beak. In doing so, he would then become an acclaimed snipe hunter.

As a naïve kid and just wanting to be accepted by his peers, Brother Oliver fell for this nasty trick. Keeping true to the ritual, the bullies secretly returned to town and left Brother Oliver alone out in the woods, where no snipe exist. By the time Brother Oliver discovered what had happened and then trudged back home, gossip had already been spread around town about his blunder. Hearing this episode, I realized that my experiences with Boone were far from unique.

While sharing his Snipe hunt story, Brother Oliver began drawing something on his sketch pad. After finishing this artwork, he tore the page from his pad and handed it to me. "This," he said, "is for you." With that, I looked upon the drawing of a dream catcher, showcasing the same symbol as I had seen in the mine shaft. "You mean this is mine to keep?" I wrote down. "YES" Brother Oliver replied, "And when I have more time, I will someday sketch you a portrait of Sage."

Throughout our conversations, I really wanted to ask Brother Oliver about his wartime experiences. However, by doing so, I feared putting him into a situation of recalling some sad chapters. Still, a part of me just wanted to say to Brother Oliver how much I admired him for serving his country. Grandpa Nutter had mentioned something about Brother Oliver deserving a Purple Heart medal for his combat injuries and I so badly wanted to know if he had ever gotten this commendation.

When first meeting someone, I always try to be careful not to ask too many questions or take up too much of their time. Having this in mind, I noted to Sage that we should now leave and allow Brother Oliver the serenity he sought here in the Church Window. With the dream catcher sketch rolled up in my hand, Sage and I bid this monk farewell. As we turned to head up the nearby ridge, Brother Oliver called out to me, "By the way Vandy, word has it you are quite the bronc-buster. Just like you, I always wanted to be a rootin' tootin' cowboy." Laughing to himself, Brother Oliver waved us goodbye, sat down once again on the forest floor, and then resumed his meditation.

During these past few weeks, I had now become acquainted with a most unusual owl, a small wonder Indian, and reclusive robed man, all of whom seemed somehow strangely connected within these woods. And as for me, I too was also becoming more and more connected to this enclave of shady hollows and shadowy characters.

As Sage and I parted from Brother Oliver, I could not help but wonder what lay ahead. My imagination no longer had any limits. Grandpa Nutter's stories no longer seemed so far-fetched. And now becoming more and more okay as otherwise, my idea of being an isolated misfit no longer seemed to apply.

# MOONSHINE SADIE

---

*Being unique is something we all have in common. Adapting to this uniqueness is what differentiates each of us.*

---

here are a whole lot of folks around here who think they know Sadie, but few really do. Most describe her as that kooky old lady living just beyond the northeast outskirts of town. Hardly anyone ever greets Sadie, bothers to talk with her, or even tries to find out much about this elderly woman. Instead, there seems to be a preference that she remains mysterious and misunderstood. That by itself makes for good gossip and strange tales. I myself have to admit to being just as guilty in believing all the scary stories about Sadie and passing them along. However, a wise old owl has now taught me to do otherwise.

Several times during my visits to Sage, I have noticed a meandering shadowy figure near the ridge of the Raggedy Oak. Slightly hunched over and skulking about, this lone wanderer seemed to be searching in the woods. Moving ever so slowly, each step by this seeker seemed precise and methodical. Dressed shabbily and appearing stout, it was hard to tell from a distance, whether this was a man or a woman. With hair tucked underneath it, a funny sort of hat covered up much of this person's face. Curious as I was about this character, I dared not venture too near. Instead, I one day asked Sage what he knew of this searcher and who it might be.

As usual, Sage knew about everyone and everything within these woods. The person I had inquired about was none other than the hometown elder often referred to as Moonshine Sadie. Sage preferred to call her Mushroom Sadie because of her frequent forages into the woods for mushrooms. According to Sage, it was during one of her mushroom hunts that the two of them met years ago. Upon becoming close friends, Sage introduced Sadie to all the hidden places where the best mushrooms grow. In return, Sadie shared with him secrets of the past such as the location of the mine we had recently uncovered.

Based on what Sage learned from Sadie, she was an only child who got orphaned by one of the local epidemics. Following the deaths of her parents, Sadie's grandparents, Henry and Bess, then took her in. Henry had been a toiling miner for many years and eventually turned to moonshining as a much more lucrative way of earning a living. As a youngster, Sadie helped to run the moonshine still and occasionally deliver jugs of this hooch. After the death of her grandfather, Sadie and her grandmother tried to continue the moonshine business, yet were stopped from doing so by a local group of feisty church ladies belonging to the Christian Women's Temperance League. These God-faring prohibitionists even threatened to burn down Sadie's home if she continued the corn mash distillery. These zealous women meant business and had already succeeded in banning the sale of any liquor within the town limits.

For decades, Sadie has lived alone in the cabin built by Henry. Decrepit and unpainted, this shelter has faded into a weathered gray shack. There are folks around here who call this rustic pioneer building an eyesore and want it demolished, just in the same way which regrettably ended the historic stone Opera House that once graced the community's main street. Wanting progress rather than preservation, some folks around here have become too anxious to label old things as blight and tear them down.

Sadie's humble haven is void of modern day utilities such as electricity, indoor plumbing, and telephone lines. An ancient outhouse is located about twenty yards behind this dwelling. The nearby wood shed stores the place's only source for heating and cooking. A forlorn iron hand pump supplies the daily water. Surrounding this homestead is a scattering of trees, bushes, and tall grass. What lies within the walls of this house remains known only to its sole occupant.

Just as Sage ended his story of this renowned hometown spinster, he paused, looked at me, and then said, "Perhaps instead of me rambling about Sadie, you should meet her yourself next week. Like you, like I, like Tustis, and like Brother Oliver, she too is otherwise."

By now, I was getting use to introductions by Sage. When the next week came around, I found myself once again following a quick stepping Sage to another destination. Because this was a time of mushroom gathering, especially for morals, Sage assured me that we would find Sadie out and about on a nearby ridge. Just as we approached that ridge, I saw the familiar shadowy figure in the distance. As Sage and I moved closer to this person, I began to identify an aged woman whose face was marked by timelines and partially covered by a gray knit cap. Her frame was stout, yet sort of hunched over from either a deformity or possibly too many years of laboring. When this lady looked directly toward me, I then could see what appeared to be the somber eyes of a forlorn soul. For the very first time, I was about to meet face to face with a notorious local legend.

Prior to today's encounter, Sage advised me that Sadie has an unusual syndrome called a tic. As such, her facial muscles repeatedly twitch. Some folks consider this batty and make fun of Sadie for something she cannot control. Sadie also talks in a very peculiar way because of a lisp. Due to a birth defect, it is quite difficult for her to pronounce certain words and speak with ease. I guess this is what one refers to as a speech impediment. Her haphazard lineup of crooked teeth only worsens this situation. Based on this manner of speaking, Sadie is often misjudged as being slow and dimwitted. Sage insisted however, that Sadie is quite the opposite and one of the most knowledgeable persons about the culture and history of this region.

Just like Brother Oliver, all my premonitions about Sadie were based on the nasty gossip of local tongue-waggers. Due to her advanced age and appearance, many cast Sadie as scary and sinister. Her reclusive nature and past ties to moonshining only added to an unsettling characterization. Most of us just wanted to believe that she was this spooky old lady near the outskirts of town. Some of the older kids even tried frightening the younger ones with tales of Sadie being a homegrown witch.

Upon spotting Sage and I, Sadie motioned for us to come forward. Pointing to her basket on the ground, she spoke out in a garbled voice, "Come see what I have found today." In the basket was a bounty of morals, some of the most prized mushrooms in this area. I could immediately sense from her expressions and tone of voice, how excited she felt about her day's foraging. Turning her gaze away from the basket and then toward me, Sadie noted, "You must be Vandy. Sage tells me that you and I have many things in common."

Now in such close proximity to this storied lady, I began to see a clearer picture of her. She stood no more than four and a half feet tall. Sadie's round face was accented by an oversized nose and prominent chin. Poking out from behind her tasseled hat was a short braid of silvery hair. Her ruddy and wrinkled complexion betrayed any remaining remnants of youth. If all the lines etched on Sadie's face were anything equivalent to rings on a tree trunk, she most certainly represented a woman of numerous decades. When watching Sadie move to and fro however, nothing about her resembled a frail elder. She seemed sturdy, strong, and limber as well.

Sadie's short and muscular fingers gave her hands the appearance of bear paws. The extremely wide and worn out high-top boots beneath this gal showcased another set of hefty paws, which had obviously endured many treks. For some reason, I fully expected her to be shy and apprehensive, yet instead, she soon came across as quite assertive. Although awkward in her conversations, Sadie had no obvious reservations about chatting and speaking her mind. As for me, I just quietly stood tight-lipped while studying this enthralling lady.

Breaking my bashful silence she spoke out and said, "I understand that you are being raised by your grandfather. That makes us kindred spirits of sorts." As we sat down on the forest floor, Sadie began sharing with me about what it was like to be raised by her paternal grandparents Henry and Bess. As for Henry, she referred to him as beloved Granpappy.

Although Henry's last name was originally Polkinghorn, it got shortened to just Horn after his Cornish parents immigrated to the United States from the Cornwall area of Great Britain. Sadie was only eleven when both her parents fell victim to a deadly epidemic and she then went to live with Henry and Bess. When Sadie began talking about her grandfather and his gift for storytelling, it almost seemed as if she was describing my Grandpa Nutter.

Sadie noted that as a youngster, she explored these woods much like I do today. Sadie also shared that these woods often served as a haven from kids who frequently teased and picked on her at the one-room schoolhouse that she attended over half a century ago. Even the tiny country church, to which Sadie had once belonged, had its share of tormenters. As a youth, Sadie lamented how hard it was to get involved in many activities when some kids either shied away or laughed at her. Because of her last name and speech difficulty, Sadie recollected how one mean-spirited kid called her a "Horn out of tune". This really reminded me of a kid I know.

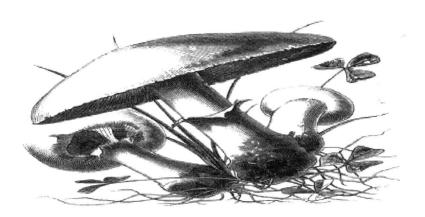

While listening to this gal, I began to understand what Sage meant when he said that Sadie and I had so much in common. I also began quickly seeing how misjudged this person was by others. Rather than being scary, Sadie seemed gentle, trusting, and understanding. Before this day was to end, I would learn even more about this astonishing lady.

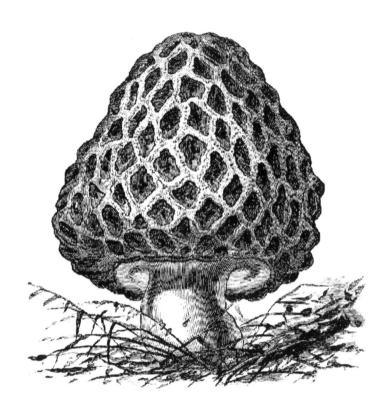

As Sadie paused for a moment, I looked over at her huge basket of mushrooms. Though not being any kind of expert on these plants, I could easily tell that they were morels. Unlike your typical toadstools with their domed canopies, these morels were pitted and sponge-like in appearance. While many folks rave about eating this weird looking fungus, neither Grandpa Nutter nor I care for mushrooms. In fact, Grandpa Nutter calls them the food of forest trolls.

Attempting to be polite and show my respect to Sadie, I remarked to her, "Sage tells me that you know more about mushrooms than anyone else." Sadie then smiled and answered, "Most of what I know about mushrooms and everything edible in these woods, I have learned from both Sage and Granpappy. As for collecting mushrooms, I must warn you to be ever so careful about whom you talk to. Mushrooms, like those morels in my basket, are highly prized by mushroom hunters. Finding them can result in feuds, fights, and even murder!" That last comment really caught my attention. "What do mean by murder?" I asked. Staring at the ground for a few moments and then looking up at me, Sadie then replied, "Apparently you have not been told about the mushroom murder in Hunter's Hollow. With this said, Sadie repeated to me a tale told to her by Granpappy Henry.

Just northwest of this park is a heavily forested area known as Hunter's Hollow. It lies within Wyoming Valley. Several generations ago, an eccentric homesteader named Josiah Sammers, owned a good portion of this land. Like many during this era, old man Sammers did not want anyone pilfering from his property. Not only did he post no trespassing signs, yet also set hidden traps around his property. Well-known at this time was a local family called the Dank brothers. They were a lawless bunch who paid no heed to signs or property rights. As such, this Dank family pretty much trespassed wherever and whenever they wanted too. Their confrontations with Mr. Sammers turned into an intense feud. After stepping into one of Sammers' traps and injuring his foot, a wounded Dank brother pledged to get even with Mr. Sammers. Several weeks later, Mr. Sammers was found fatally shot in his woods. From what the sheriff could ascertain, the victim suffered a bullet wound to his right leg while out gathering morels and other mushrooms. In speculation, it appeared that the intention of the gunshot might have been to scare rather than to kill Mr. Sammers. Instead, as a result of this crime, the old bachelor bled to death alone out there in his woods. According to a local legend, blood red mushrooms sprout up each year in the very spot where Josiah Sammers died. Some folks will even tell you that his spirit haunts this area and frightens away those who enter it. Others claim that all mushrooms picked from this neck of the woods, now cause deadly poisoning.

Although there were strong suspicions that the Dank brothers were behind this shooting, the law authorities could not bring any culprit to justice for the ghastly murder. However, because of continuing problems with these Dank brothers, the local sheriff eventually managed to run most of the family out of the county.

With an inquisitive look, Sadie commented, "I'm not sure about all the facts associated with this murder mystery, yet I can tell you another tale that is absolutely the gospel truth. For decades, many people have searched for the wild ginseng that grows in this area. Because of the folklore surrounding its medicinal remedies, this plant is even more coveted than the morels. After discovering a sizable patch years ago, I began harvesting these ginseng roots and storing them in my cellar. One afternoon, I heard a loud knock at my door. Upon opening it, there stood an Asian man, wearing a dress suit and carrying a briefcase. The only word this unusual visitor could speak clearly to me that I understood was "ginseng", which he repeated over and over. This annoyance eventually made me give in. In response to his insistence, I retrieved all the ginseng roots that I had recently gathered. When I showed him my

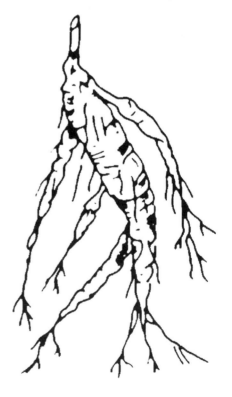

harvest, his eyes opened widely. He then carefully examined each and every root. Shaking his head in approval, this stranger next reached into his briefcase, sorted out a handful of cash, and then rewarded me with a considerable number of American dollars. Taking the ginseng from me, he walked back to his fancy car and quickly drove away. Since then, this same man has shown up each year at a similar time and repeated this exchange. To date, I know nothing about the Oriental man, his name, or where he hails from. Most of all, I have no idea on how he came to learn about my ginseng. What I do know however, is that his coming and going from my place has only added to all the jabbering gossip about me."

Sadie said that after consulting with Tustis about her ginseng encounters, he reflected on a past meeting with a Chinaman, who like him, was also a shaman. This Asian spiritual man and healer shared with Tustis that his culture had collected and prescribed ginseng for thousands of years. Eventually, this cherished commodity got overharvested in the Far East, and as such, ambitious buyers from the Orient now venture to this country in diligent search of ginseng. What these searchers covet the most are roots that take on the appearance of a man's body. Due to long held beliefs, these human-figured roots are alleged to contain even more potent properties. Sadie remarked that she had twice discovered roots with this eerie shape to them.

Hearing these unusual tales from Sadie, I wondered what other fascinating stories she had to share. When I asked Sadie what she could tell me about the old mine shaft now being occupied by Sage, her response caught me off guard. "I understand that you are curious about the markings in Granpappy's old mine," Sadie remarked. "As such, I have something else to show you today at my home."

Looking to Sage, he gave me a wink of assurance. He had known beforehand that I would be invited to Sadie's place and anticipated my surprise. "Although not being able to join you today on your trek near town, I most certainly will be interested in the outcome," said Sage. With that, Sage turned and headed back toward his mineshaft home, while leaving me somewhat marooned alongside this mysterious lady. I had trusted Sage's judgment before and would now cautiously do the same again. With Sadie leading the way, I followed along.

It took about forty-five minutes to reach Sadie's home. For someone long in the tooth, Sadie maintained a steady pace. I sometimes found myself struggling to keep up with this elder. Along the way, all was silent except for a tune being hummed by Sadie. When I finally interrupted to ask her about this tune, she noted that it was an old Cornish folksong, taught to her by Granpappy Henry. I then told her that this song reminded me of a similar tune played by my grandfather on his harmonica.

Without elaborating any further about this tune, Sadie lifted her arm and pointed forward at a couple of structures just ahead of us. "Welcome to my place," Sadie announced. At this point, I will admit to having goose bumps. Nobody I knew had ever come this close to Sadie's place. After stepping onto her property, it almost felt like I was entering a time machine. The old cabin built by her grandfather was a relic of pioneer days. Guarded on its north side by towering trees and tall grass, this homestead stood partially concealed from the main road. A huge tree

sprouted from its front porch. An attached and decaying storeroom tilted badly. Adjacent to this house stood a ramshackle building. An axe and huge wood pile could be seen alongside this shed. A vintage cast iron hand pump appeared rusted into the landscape. An enormous garden and prickly raspberry patch lay cultivated on the south side. Near them were boxlike structures which housed beehives. Just beyond this area, several groves of smaller trees formed an orchard. Grape vines contorted around a sagging arbor. And farther back on the property, the venerable outhouse remained in servitude. With all of these things added together, it was evident how Sadie sustained herself.

From the sights and sounds, it became readily apparent that Sadie nurtured the songbirds around her. Everywhere I looked, birds were either straddling branches or fluttering to and fro. Their movements created a constantly changing kaleidoscope of colors and contrasts. An endless chorus of singing, chirping, whistling, shrieking, and even an occasional caw filled the air. Although a setting of solitude, this place was certainly not one of silence. At one point, I even spotted a blue jay, which suspiciously resembled Snitch.

From what I had been told, no one dared to set foot, for any length of time, on this lady's isolated property. What I now endeavored, would mark me as either the bravest or most foolish. Sadie was often touted as wielding a shotgun when trespassers approached. The local peeping Toms, who sometimes chided each other to get a close up, would only dash a hesitant short distance down the road leading to Sadie's home. Even the most persistent panhandling hobos shied away from this place.

My teenage imagination spun wildly as I began to tread cautiously around this hallowed place. Having entered such an unbelievable realm, pounding heartbeats were echoing in my ears and seemed to be drowning out all the bird calls. Facing the doorway and attempting to step onto the porch, my awkward legs suddenly felt extremely heavy and uncooperative. Returning to an old habit of mine, I just froze until a voice spoke out and broke this spell. "Although none of these surroundings are much to look at, please come in," said Sadie. "I have something quite interesting to show you." Entering through the old weathered doorway, it took several minutes for my eyes to adjust within the dimly lit interior. Dangling from the ceiling were a couple of kerosene lanterns, one of which Sadie immediately lighted.

From what I could see, the inside was comprised of two rooms. The main room which I now stood in had little more than a table, three chairs, small rocker, and wood burning stove. Crowded on the table were baskets and canning jars. Atop the wood burning stove sat several cast iron kettles. Against one wall was an old hutch with a broom stationed beside it. Near the opposite wall was an unusual stockpile which appeared to include a shotgun, statue, baskets, buckets, crocks, and an antique mantel clock resting on an old oak barrel.

Seeing that I was staring at these items, Sadie said to me, "Most of those things once belonged to a man called Wild Bill. They were given to Grandpa Henry as payment for moonshine. And in that barel sitting there, is what I want to show you."

Walking across the creaking wood floor of this room, Sadie approached the stockpile. She then lifted the clock off the barrel, removed the barrel's round top, and peered inside. "Come here and look," she commanded. Feeling both curious and uneasy, I followed her instructions by pacing toward this barrel. With a little reluctance, I peeked inside. Completely startled, a huge owl face stared back at me. "That's the same symbol from the mine shaft and Brother Oliver's dream catcher. What's it doing in there?" I asked. Sadie just eyed me over and replied, "According to my friend Tustis, you are the one to uncover that secret!"

At this point, I was totally unclear as to what Sadie meant. I saw no connection between myself and the strange owl symbols. All I knew about them was the story told to me by Tustis. Still curious about all this, I asked Sadie if she knew anything about the other markings in her grandfather's mine. Although Sadie had no information relating to the beast symbol, she did have a story to tell about the sign of the Oakist. Sadie shared that the Oakist is often considered nothing more than a fabled Indian tale. She, however, had actually come to know several of them. When I asked if Sadie could introduce me to an Oakist, she rebuffed my request by saying that an Oakist cannot be revealed through another and instead must be individually discovered by one's self. Sadie then quickly ended this particular conversation after telling me that I had most likely met an Oakist during my previous ventures through the nearby woods.

As I stood wondering about all these bewildering revelations, Sadie indicated that she had something else to show me. From the old hutch she then retrieved a leather case of sorts. As Sadie opened this case, I saw what appeared to be a collection of papers. The one on top showcased the sketch of a gray haired man with a hat and long sideburns. "That's Grandpa Henry," Sadie said. "Tustis refers to him as a *squitawaboo* man, which is a Chippewa word meaning firewater."

Lifting this first sketch off the top, Sadie began showing me the rest of the drawings. Most of these sketches seemed to be of Native American scenes. One of the most intriguing drawings was that of an elder Indian smoking a pipe. Sadie noted that this particular man was named Talon and had been a close friend of her grandfather. Another of these interesting sketches showcased a bearded man donning a wide-brimmed hat, who struck an uncanny resemblance to Grandpa Nutter. "That's Sheriff Morey", said Sadie. "He pretty much ruled the roost in these parts and protected Granpappy Henry's business, even though this lawman was a teetotaler and never touched a drop of liquor. Sometimes Sheriff Morey got criticized by local folks as an Indian sympathizer. However, any troublemaker knew better than to cross paths with this sheriff. After Granpappy died, Sheriff Morey became like another grandfather by watching over Grandma Bess and me." Reflecting back on one of Sadie's stories, I then asked, "Isn't he the same sheriff that ran off the

Dank brothers in your mushroom murder tale?" Seeming pleased that I had recounted her story, Sadie replied with a broad smile, "I'm really glad that you pay attention to the tales told by this old lady."

The last of the sketches was the only one portraying a woman. It showed her standing in the entryway to a home. Seeing that I was puzzled by this picture, Sadie spoke up and said, "That drawing is a mystery to me as well. Grandma Bess referred to her as Cousin Edna and sighed that she had died in a tragic boating accident. While fishing with her husband, a sudden wind overturned the boat. She drowned in the big river north of here, even though her husband desperately tried to save her, he almost drowned as well. Afterwards, this sad disaster caused all kinds of turmoil in the family."

Sadie explained that these sketches were drawn by a reclusive hermit known as Wild Bill. In his will, Wild Bill designated that all of his artwork go to Granpappy Henry. This inherited art represented Wild Bill's gratitude for regular deliveries of moonshine. Only once had Sadie accompanied her grandfather to Wild Bill's place. It was located just north of where I now live with Grandpa Nutter. According to Sadie, Wild Bill earned his nickname from a well-established reputation of ranting and raving whenever anyone trespassed onto his property. Oftentimes he did so while under the influence of Granpappy Henry's moonshine. When sober however, Wild Bill spent most of his time drawing and painting at his isolated homestead. Apart from his contact with Granpappy and just a few other locals, Wild Bill preferred his hermit lifestyle and wanted little to do with anyone else. Most area residents consented by avoiding this strange artist, who rarely exited his home without carrying a loaded double-barreled shotgun. What Sadie seemed to remember most about Wild Bill was his funny looking hat, long thin face, scraggly sideburns, and bloodshot eyes.

Sadie's grandfather shared with her that Wild Bill had not always been an ornery sort of character. Tragedy and hard times in his life had changed him. For many years, Bill was revered as the area's water witch. Quite successful at the ritual of dowsing, Bill located sites for local farmers and others to dig their wells. This popular practice of the era consisted of carrying a forked stick, usually cut from a peach tree or willow.

Holding onto the two extended forks and walking about with the shaft held parallel to the earth, a water witch slowly searched about for underground pools. Once discovered, the shaft would begin pointing directly toward the location beneath it. This area then got staked off and dug out until water was reached. Certain gifted folks like Bill, seemed to have a natural affinity for this activity. Highly regarded and often sought after, rarely did Wild Bill ever fail in his dowsing pursuits. However, there suddenly came a day when he gave up this practice and everything else to become a hermit.

OWL

OWL

OWL

OWL

It was unknown to Sadie what had actually happened to Bill that sent him into seclusion. From looking at the sketches, his artistic talent certainly became apparent. Each of these drawings seemed to tell a tale of the times. Although Sadie had done such a good job of preserving these art pieces, I could not help but think that Wild Bill's work deserved greater recognition.

Taking another look at all these drawings, I noticed something peculiar that had been written in the lower right hand corner of each sketch. Turning to Sadie, I asked, "Why has he written the word OWL beneath each drawing?" Sadie sort of snickered and replied, "I had to ask Granpappy the same thing. Although it looks like the word owl, it is actually the artist's signature. Wild Bill's full name was Oliver William Lucas, and therefore, his initials spell out as OWL."

In a moment of confusion, my mind suddenly flashed back to the conversation I had with Brother Oliver about the mysterious owl sketches that show up each year at the local American Legion Hall. These too include the word OWL written on the bottom of each sketch. Everyone assumed that this was just a simple title for each owl drawing. Although I had come to suspect that Brother Oliver was in some way connected to the owl drawings, there now seemed to be a possible connection to Wild Bill as well. Because Brother Oliver and Wild Bill were generations apart, this made no sense at all.

"Sometimes on a rainy day," said Sadie, "I look at these drawings just to remember days in the past." Before closing up the case of sketches, I noticed a number of documents stacked beneath these drawings. Becoming perhaps a bit too nosey, I asked Sadie about these other papers. In response, she became clearly defensive in her tone of voice and answered, "Those are just some old mining claims, deeds and a few other papers that you need not concern yourself with." Sadie then immediately closed the leather case and returned it to the hutch. Though I knew better than to pry further, my curiosity now heightened over these documents and the drawings as well. I also could not help wondering as to whatever became of this artist named Wild Bill.

Everything about this elder named Sadie seemed intriguing. That included her appearance, her surroundings, and the stories she had to tell. Listening to her life's tales and sitting within this old miner's cabin made me feel as if I had stepped into a past era. Just as I was getting ready to depart, Sadie entertained me with another surprise. Walking toward the center of the room, Sadie bent over and rolled back a braided rug. Underneath it was a trap door. Pulling the door open, Sadie then signaled for me to come and look below. Feeling somewhat squeamish, I hesitated a bit before glancing into this dark chamber. Not knowing all I needed to about this eccentric lady, what lay below was anyone's guess.

From the kerosene lantern hanging nearby, a flicker of its light seemed to be reflecting off something within this earthy smelling root cellar. Straining the best I could, I saw what appeared to be a huge copper tub and tubing. Before I had time to figure this out, Sadie proudly proclaimed, "That's Granpappy's moonshine still, which by the way, can be made operable if need be. The tub is known as a turnip pot and those condensing coils are called a worm. Most of what his still produced got sold to nearby nip joints, one of which was that old Higbee Hotel in town. It had a secret backroom, referred to as a speakeasy. You had to be of some importance, just to get in and share a nip or two. Mind you, not all of Granpappy's moonshine got served to snobbish snoots. Adding some honey and cherry juice, the corner drug store bottled it as cough syrup. Mixed with camphor, it was also sold as a rub-on headache remedy. There was even a local merchant who travelled about and hawked this moonshine as Dr. Swill's Magic Elixir, a cure-all for everything afflicting you. And of course, Granpappy had his special customers, such as Wild Bill. I really miss those days of helping Granpappy and have often thought about resurrecting his trade. Of course young man, you need not mention this still or Granpappy's exploits to anyone else."

While Sadie chuckled about the prospect of reviving this sacred corn-mash and yeast contraption, I experienced the chilled feeling that perhaps the spiritual presence of Granpappy Henry remained alongside this moonshine machinery. I continued to feel unsettled until Sadie finally closed the trap door and place the rug over it. Because my ghoulish imagination had now been stirred, I got this notion in my head that her Granpappy Henry might be buried in this same root cellar. Being perhaps too curious and taking a chance, I just had to ask Sadie, "What became of your Granpappy?" In response Sadie answered, "He died of a heart ailment while in his eighties and is forever buried alongside my grandmother at unmarked sites near the Old Rock Church." Hearing this, I had to ask, "You mean the cemetery next to where Brother Oliver lives?" Sadie then replied, "You are right, and by the way, that is how I came to meet Brother Oliver while visiting my grandparents' graves."

Delving into this subject, Sadie went on to remark that she had no idea as to where her parents were buried. She noted that during the era when her parents passed on, it was not unusual for folks to die young from cholera, smallpox, flu, scarlet fever, tuberculosis, diphtheria, and other diseases. These widespread ailments kept many folks of her parents and grandparents generations, from reaching the age of forty. Becoming orphaned seemed all too commonplace. Having relatives such as Henry and Bess to take her in, Sadie considered herself more fortunate than most.

Knowing of the long hike ahead of me, Sadie stated that I probably now needed to start trekking back to my home. Assuring me that I was welcome to her place at any time, Sadie then indicated that we would be meeting again soon. Somehow, this notation seemed more like a premonition than a farewell exchange. During my walk back through the woods, I kept thinking about this elderly spinster and how she had survived on her own for so many years. It saddened me to think that Sadie most likely spends each Christmas, Thanksgiving, and even her own birthday, all alone. Had she ever listened to a radio, watched television, or heard about that new rock & roll band called the Beatles? Has she ever licked a strawberry ice cream cone from the Corner Drug store, sipped a cherry Coke at Kelly's soda fountain, or chomped on buttered popcorn at the Dodge movie house? Did she ever get to play with a Slinky, build a Lincoln Logs cabin, assemble a creepy Cootie, or swing at a whiffle ball? What would her everyday life be like if Sadie could just simply flick a switch and have lighting in her home or turn on a faucet for hot water? Thinking about all of this, I suddenly came to realize just how lucky my life really is.

Part of me admired Sadie immensely, yet I continued to be slightly skittish about this character. Based on all the past stories gossiped about her, I had to overcome a prejudice of my own and acquaint myself with the real Sadie. This meant understanding the lonely life she has endured after losing both her parents and grandparents. It also meant realizing the taunting and teasing got bestowed upon her because of a haggard appearance, hunchback profile, and garbled voice. What seemed strangest of all however, was this kinship feeling of being oddly connected to Sadie and fascinated by her incredible wisdom and gentle nature.

After returning home today, my encounter with Sadie remained a secret. Nonetheless, I began peppering Grandpa Nutter with questions about this lady. I wanted to know everything that he knew relating to her. Before any of that, I needed to quiz him about the Mushroom Murder. "Grandpa," I asked, "What can you tell me about the mushroom murder in Hunters' Hollow?"

Seemingly caught off guard by my question, Grandpa raised his eyebrows and began rubbing his whiskered chin. After a short period of reflection, he replied, "Heavens to Betsy, now that there is a tale I had not thought of for a long, long, time." With this said, Grandpa Nutter then repeated to me almost the exact story told by Sadie.

Sensing my interest in this tale, Grandpa looked at me and noted, "Perhaps you need to hear another connection to this story. Remember our first hike into the woods and how I showed you that old abandoned car? It supposedly belonged to the youngest Dank brother. After being booted out of the county, he crossed state lines and got involved with one of the infamous Chicago gangsters. Attempting to lay low for a while, he drove back here to hide out at his sister's farm. Being tipped off, the local cops were waiting for him when he arrived in town. As a chase ensued, this Dank brother headed out this way and tried to escape the police by driving down an old logging road. His car eventually got stuck and abandoned. Following a manhunt of several days, this fugitive got cornered, just after nightfall, down by the river. Rather than surrender, he jumped into the currents and was never seen again.

When Grandpa finished, I then inquired as to whether any of the Dank family still remains in this area. "The only one I know of," said Grandpa, "is a lady who just happens to be the grandmother to that kid you call Boone." Somewhat shocked, I looked sternly at Grandpa Nutter and exclaimed, "You mean to tell me that Boone is a relative of the Dank brothers!" Caught again in another moment of recollection, Grandpa answered, "It's more than likely that one of the Dank brothers in the mushroom murder story was his great grandfather. Now tell me, just how did you get to be so curious about this local legend?" Protecting my source, I simply responded that a friend had mentioned this story and some tales about Sadie as well.

Without dithering, Grandpa Nutter responded that there is far more to Sadie Horn than most folks realize. Grandpa said that because of Sadie's quirky appearance and the shabby old cabin she lives in, some area residents consider her a local blight and have attempted to force Sadie out of the area. Based on a lot of hearsay and foolish nonsense, many are just plain scared of her. There are also several longtime upstanding residents who see Sadie as an embarrassing reminder that their past relatives heavily patronized her grandfather's moonshine operation and even borrowed money from him to start many of the town's present day businesses. And what many keep tight lipped about is the fact that Sadie, by way of her inheritance from Henry Horn, actually holds the deeds to a number of properties on which these businesses were built. No one dares to discuss what would happen should Sadie decide to legally lay claim to these lands. Even the old slag furnace in town, which city officials have designated as a historical site, actually sits upon land owned by Sadie. What is still more worrisome to these officials is that Sadie reputedly holds age-old leases pertaining to the locations of the City Hall, one of the local banks, and a popular tavern. To keep on Sadie's good side, some merchants routinely drop off supplies to her home.

Grandpa Nutter cautioned me that Sadie was not as vulnerable as many think. Should anyone attempt to uproot this lady, she has a considerable number of influential allies and advocates who have pledged to assist her. Without going into any further details, Grandpa Nutter paused a bit and asked me point blank, "How come you have taken such a sudden interest in this quaint old gal?" I then paused as well and sheepishly answered, "After seeing her several times rummaging around in the woods, I just wondered who she really was and whether all the stories about her were true." Grandpa Nutter leaned back in his chair, placed his hand upon his whiskered chin once again, and thoughtfully replied, "Just like you, I often wonder too."

# TROUBLESHOOTERS

---

*As long as you maintain your aim, it does not
matter where your sights are set*

---

pon entering the woods this morning, I could sense that something was suspiciously wrong. A thick fog dangled throughout the hollows and made visibility difficult. In a patchwork masquerade, Mother Nature seemed to be playing a game of hide and seek. What really caught my attention was the ruckus being made by the yacking crows. Such a huge gathering of these featherbrained critters usually signals some kind of trouble in the forest. Their obnoxious calls were echoing from one tree to another. My first thought concerned Sage. Were these crows ganging up and picking on him again? Or perhaps, something even more sinister was now impending.

Quite often on my routine hikes, I've heard these crows milling about and constantly cawing. They seem to be nature's bigmouthed busybodies. Grandpa Nutter calls them scavenging trash talkers. Tustis once told me that crows are the wayward spirits which have yet to cross over. Maybe I should have more respect for these babblers, yet to me, crows are just plain annoying.

Although sighting and hearing crows was a common occurrence, this particular time felt different. The incredible number of crows and their series of calls were more than I had ever witnessed. The ranting messages being communicated to each other were intense and frantic. As I ventured farther on, one of Tustis's proverbs flashed before me. In a tree at the edge of the woods were four crows perched side by side. In learning to read the forest, Tustis advised me that seeing the rare sight of three or more crows perched on the same tree branch, indicates a sign of forthcoming trouble. With all these frenzied featherheads squawking about, I grew ever more wary of whatever had gotten them so riled.

Most of the nerve-racking routine seemed to be coming from an area dubbed the "Broken Woods". During a stormy wind blast of three years ago, half the trees within this grove crashed down and created a shambled enclave within the forest. This haphazard tangle of shredded branches and tree trunks formed a sheltered hideout for anything wanting to be left alone. If any bear, wildcat, or other suspected beast existed in these woods, this certainly would be its domain. Based on the past howls I have heard coming from within this entangled windfall, there appears to be a pack of coyotes residing here. For the most part, I cautiously stay away from this eerie area and view it from a distance.

Doing my best to move quickly, I hurried awkwardly toward Sage's mineshaft den. This was again one of those frustrating times when I desperately wished I could run hard and fast like other kids, yet my misfit legs would not cooperate. Being ever so careful to hold back and maintain my balance, I could not afford to take a treacherous tumble at this time. Crossing my fingers, I kept hoping that Sage was not in any kind of mortal danger.

Despite all my efforts to tread cautiously, the forest floor I now contended with was considerably slippery from the fog condensing upon it. While traversing down a steep grade, I suddenly lost my footing on the carpet of wet leaves and began a harrowing nosedive. Happening so quickly, I did not even have time to plant my walking stick and recover any balance. Twisting to adjust my landing, I then flopped onto the ground and rolled sideways for several feet. As I brushed wet leaves and grass off myself, a small shadowy figure approached me from my left. I sort of froze at first, while straining to peer through the fog. With both hands clutched to my walking stick, I took a defensive stance and prepared for battle. As the diminishing fog cleared just enough to uncover the approaching entity, I then recognized a familiar voice calling out to me. "About time you arrived," said Sage. "There are troubleshooters in the forest and we've got to act fast. And by the way, that was quite an impressive arrival on your part!"

Looking at my friend Sage, I then asked, "Is that why the crows are all stirred up this morning?" "Yes" answered Sage, who then began explaining the reason for the chaotic sound-offs. Snitch had just flown in to alert Sage that two poachers had now entered the woods. They were bizarrely clad and carried weapons. These armed strangers seemed to be staggering about while squabbling loudly. The crows had already sensed them as a dangerous lot. Worst of all, they had just passed by the Broken Woods and were headed in this direction.

Based on a tale told to me by Sadie, a chilling thought now crossed my mind. Are these the vagabond gypsies I had been warned about? According to Sadie, there was a time not long ago, when colorfully festooned gypsies frequented this area. Once or twice a year, these wanderers from faraway places named Bulgaria, Romania, and Hungary, would venture into this community and set off an anxious frenzy among the local citizenry. Labeling the gypsies as thieves and beggars, many folks would lock their gates and doors. Fearing they might be kidnapped, children were sternly instructed to remain in their homes and dare not to even get a peak at these strangers. Any garden produce and other items of value were quickly gathered and stored away. Even the family dogs got fetched into the home and safeguarded from capture. Shopkeepers were incredibly wary of gypsies and oftentimes closed up their stores when the call went out "the gypsies are coming!"

Sadie claimed that like a lot of people, gypsies are often misunderstood. Similar to the hobos who use to hang out in the rail yards, she said that gypsies travel about as free spirits. Although some have been accused of stealing for a living, many represent flamboyant entertainers who show off juggling skills, read palms, perform exotic dances, and play rousing squeezebox music. There were times, when Granpappy's moonshine somehow got into their camps and eventually created a need for intervention by Sheriff Morey. Meandering from one town to the next in their gaudy dress and horse drawn wagons, they often acted like fog, by unexpectedly showing up and then just as quickly disappearing. And unfortunately, there were times when local possessions disappeared with them as well.

While the gypsy women adorned themselves with layered skirts, bright scarves, huge hoop earrings, and numerous dangling bracelets, the men clad themselves in wool vests, balloon-sleeved shirts, broad leather belts, and baggy trousers tucked into high top-boots. One particular gypsy family was led by an elderly matriarch known as "Toothless Tashanda". Considered a sorceress, Tashanda got sought out by desperate persons needing to rid themselves of a curse or bad luck. Mysteries and embellished tales always surrounded Tashanda and the other gypsies. At the county fair, a gypsy called Brulando showed up one year with a captive bear. With an enormous chain wrapped around its neck, the bear got led from its cage and made to dance as an audience gathered. However, it was later learned, that another gypsy pickpocketed the onlookers during this performance.

Seeing that Sage was quite concerned about these current intruders, I asked, "Are these gypsies in our woods?" Appearing surprised by my inquiry, Sage replied, "Likely not. Most gypsies travel in caravans along established roads." Still trying to impress Sage with my insight into this situation, I then inquired, "Perhaps, these are hobos, like the ones who use to hang out at the rail yard in town." Pausing momentarily, Sage responded, "Possibly, but not probably. The two suspects now sneaking about are indubitably a much more unusual type of stranger. And for that reason, we must be precarious about this nefarious duo." Once again, Sage's way with words left me baffled.

This park and its woods were a designated wildlife refuge. Only during certain times and in limited areas were licensed hunters allowed to stalk about. Being this was midsummer, it was not the season for any kind of hunting. As such, the two figures with their weapons definitely represented despicable poachers. Although there had been poachers before in this neck of the woods, most of these critter-seeking criminals skulked about under the cover of night. The buffoons now wandering about were brashly doing so in broad daylight.

Following the lead of Snitch, Sage and I climbed toward the top of a nearby ridge. From this vantage point, we hoped to spot the unsavory hunters and see where they were heading. Sure enough, just as we crested this ridge, two figures could be seen entering at the far end of the valley below. Sage then became intensely nervous. He looked at me and said, "If those two continue toward the other end of this valley, my friend Buzz will surely be in danger. I need to go quickly and warn him. In the meantime, you must run as fast as you can and get help." In response, I said to Sage, "I'll try, but you already know what happens whenever my legs attempt to speed up." Sage then looked sternly at me and advised, "You can keep your balance and increase your pace by simply alternating your strides with one long step and them a short one. It is sort of the same thing I learned when trying to fly with one good wing. Just adapt and move on."

Although I had yet to meet Buzz, Sage oftentimes mentioned this feathered friend. Buzz is a turkey vulture, or what some call a buzzard. I've seen these gargantuan birds hovering over the far end of Twin Valley and circling about on the updrafts. Though beautiful to watch, they are ugly to view. If not for the blood red skin around their scalped heads and flabby necks, the harsh perceptions of them would lessen considerably. Of course, the drab plumage and massive hooked beaks do nothing to enhance their beauty as well. Being more like scavenger than predators, these homely critters keep everything in balance. Because these grim reapers generally show up whenever a forest dweller passes on, Grandpa refers to vultures as "flying undertakers". Based on Sage's calculations, his cherished comrade is the oldest and wisest creature in this forest. Sage claims that whenever Buzz is asked about just how old he really is, this antiquated aviator always responds by saying that he is not quite yet a dinosaur, but the closest thing to one around here. Because of this elderly status, Buzz has grown increasingly near-sighted and slow motioned. Nonetheless, this patriarchal bird resides atop one of the zombie trees and listens to everything that goes on in these woods. He can even pick up on the slightest sounds that are miles away. Guided by his keen sense of smell, Buzz detects anything carried by the wind. The clenched talons anchoring this bird to the treetops, represent a sharp reminder of threatening weaponry. And when need be, Buzz's enormous yet stiff wings, can still take to the air and create an imposing presence. Nonetheless, with hunters prowling about, this noble critter, now hobbled by time, might well become one of their targets.

Nervous and worried, I headed awkwardly back home. Because of previous mishaps, like the one earlier this morning, I usually hold back and proceed with caution. Because of the dire circumstances now at hand, time was of the essence. Trusting in Sage's advice, I began to let go and allow my legs to speed up. Although perilously bouncing back and forth, I soon found myself becoming comfortable with the increased pace. For the first time ever, I was actually running freely without stumbling and falling. Upon finally getting within sight of my home, I slowed down to catch my breath. Standing outside in the front yard was Grandpa Nutter. Immediately sensing that something seemed wrong, Grandpa Nutter began walking toward me and calling out, "What's going on young man?"

"There are poachers in the woods." I shouted. "We need to call Uncle Matt." Grandpa just nodded and without hesitation, he headed into the house to make the call. Uncle Matt serves as a deputy with the County Sheriff's Department. He is part of a family tradition whereby there has always been a member of each generation engaged in law enforcement. Whenever there is trouble and help needed, Uncle Matt responds.

While waiting for Grandpa to make the call, I crossed my fingers and hoped that Uncle Matt was available. If not, one of the town cops would have to assist. More than likely, that would be Officer Tiny, who is absolutely the opposite of his nickname. From what Grandpa claims, Officer Tiny weighs just over 400 pounds. I got acquainted with him last year while visiting a friend in town and setting off firecrackers. After someone reported the unwanted commotion, Officer Tiny showed up to give us a stern tongue lashing. Seeing this behemoth police officer exiting his squad car was more than intimidating. I doubt any other community has a policeman as enormous as the one in this town of mine. Grandpa told me that Officer Tiny had years ago been a champion prize fighter. He also said that this local cop is a master clocksmith and restored the cuckoo clock hanging in our living room. I doubt this rotund lawman could actually run down any crook on foot, but then again, he would certainly be one heck of a roadblock to get around. Perhaps, this Santa-sized policeman should consider cutting back on any patrols near the main street eateries like Crubaugh's Bakery or the Huddle Cafe.

As much as the help was needed, I did not want to again confront Officer Tiny. Fortunately, my uncle got contacted and immediately came speeding on his way. Because he had been patrolling nearby, it took only a few minutes before hearing the high-pitched-sound of an approaching siren. Moments later, a county squad car pulled into our driveway. With his window rolled down, Uncle Matt then called out to me, "Jump in and show me where the culprits are."

With the siren again blaring and lights flashing, we headed for the park office. Uncle Matt had already radioed the park ranger to meet us there. After pulling into the parking lot and exiting the squad car, Uncle Matt and I crawled into the ranger's waiting jeep. Upon noting to this park official that the poachers had been last seen near the area I call the Broken Woods, he knew exactly where to go.

Although I had never personally met this wildlife officer until now, most everyone around here referred to him as Ranger Walt. From what I have been told, his full proper name is Walter Walters. As a park policeman, Ranger Walt carries a notorious reputation for cussing out or booting out anyone found breaking the rules. After confronting a man caught trapping in the park several years ago, he chased this scoundrel for over two miles before finally treeing him. Ranger Walt then climbed the tree, tossed the man out of it, and then jumped down to arrest him. Since then, very few have dared to challenge this ranger.

Driving down an old logging road that now served as a hiking trail, it did not take long for us to reach the area just beyond the Broken Woods. As we motored up a slight grade and crested the hill, Ranger Walt suddenly slammed on the brakes. Reacting to the sudden stop, Uncle Matt exclaimed, "I'll be darned. We almost ran over Robin Hood and Little John!" Immediately in front of us were the two implicated poachers, one

carrying a long bow and the other armed with a medieval broad axe. Dressed in some sort of costumes, each wore a belted frock. One of the bearded figures donned what appeared to be a helmet, arm guards, and leggings. Instead of being startled by the fact that we had almost run them over, the poacher nearest to us simply removed his boldly feathered hat and announced, "Greetings fair citizens. Come join us on our noble hunt for the forest beast." Just by the tone of his voice and tipsy nature, it was more than evident that this guy had been drinking. The laughter being echoed by his companion indicated a similar state of intoxication. Steadying his wavering stance and gathering some composure, the oddly-attired fellow nearest to us then began introducing himself and his hunting partner by stating, "Gentlemen, I am Lord Gilroy, the Viceroy of Bellenroy, and this here is Sir Henrik, regal knight of Wickingham. As emissaries of his majesty, King Bartholomew, we have been commissioned by the crown to seek out the fearsome beast which menaces these woods and see that it is served up for the annual feast. As such, you are welcome to join us on this royal quest. And if you choose to do so, I will personally reward you with the same grog of which Sir Henrik and I have partaken."

Somewhat amused by the unusual rhetoric of this poacher, Uncle Matt responded in a mimicking manner, "And what beast would that be which ye are seeking." Almost in unison, the two poachers responded, "The wild boar."

Ranger Walt then followed suit by replying back in much the same way as Uncle Matt had done. "First of all, I must warn ye," he said, "that your commission has no jurisdiction on these grounds where no hunting is allowed. Furthermore, no wild boars or anything of the like roam these parts. And finally, it seems highly doubtful the two of you could bring down any such animal in your current conditions and with those weapons."

The man who introduced himself as Lord Gilroy instantly became agitated and retorted loudly, "Gentlemen, you most certainly disrespect our nobility and thus underestimate our accolades. Sir Henrik and I have slayed many a beast in this kingdom. We are both regal champions of the sword, lance, and joust. And when it comes to true flying arrows, I excel in archery as well"

In an attempt to show off his archer prowess, Lord Gilroy began bungling with his long bow. After notching an arrow, he drew back slowly on the bow string. "Watch closely, oh skeptical ones, as I vanquish that nearby stump," said Gilroy. Letting go, the arrow then flew in a high arch and to the far right of the stump. Landing in a patch of tall grass, a rooster pheasant suddenly exploded into the sky. Cackling loudly, it winged off in a hurried escape. "Though that stump remains safe for now, you sure did put a good scare into that pheasant!" exclaimed Ranger Walt. "Perhaps," retorted Gilroy, I did not account for the wind." However, without even a slight breeze in the air, the only hot air blowing about was that coming from Lord Gilroy. As Uncle Matt and Ranger Walt smirked at each other, it now became necessary to intervene and lay down the law. "Unfortunately for the two of you," said Ranger Walt, "this part of the kingdom is off-limits. And although I may not be the Sheriff of Nottingham, "I do have the authority to banish you from these woods. And should you fail to comply, I most certainly could have you shackled and jailed!"

Uncle Matt then interjected, "I take it that you noblemen are participating in that nearby Renaissance Faire, to which you now need to return. Otherwise, we have a local dungeon that may not be at all to your liking."

Sobered by the remarks of Uncle Matt and Ranger Walt, the two would-be hunters paused while collecting their befuddled thoughts. Finally, Lord Gilroy grumbled out, "Gentlemen, you bequeath to us a most serious dilemma and thus we relinquish our sojourning crusade. My distinguished companion and I will without haste, return at once to consult our beloved king and his regal court at Castlehurst. However, and in doing so, we now leave empty handed and warn you that without our protection and prowess, the doom and danger of the snorting beast lurks ominously within the realm of these shadowy woods."

Lord Gilroy's conciliatory speech echoed more than a mouthful. I felt somewhat torn between laughing at this comical duo and yet sympathizing with their failed quest. Needless to say, Buzz and the rest of the forest critters no longer faced any imminent danger, at least not today.

Before departing, Lord Gilroy turned to look at me and noted, "Perhaps youthful one, someday you will earn the opportunity of being a squire or ward to nobility such as I." Laughing at this commentary, Sir Henrik then bellowed out. "I should think him more suitable as a court jester". Uncle Matt reacted immediately by retorting back, "You speak like a dimwitted oaf. In these uplands, such insults of an esteemed lad merit a beheading." With his eyes wide open and beginning to bug out, Sir Henrik turned to me and said, "Noble lad, I retract what has been babbled like a dimwit. It is the grog which makes me speak so foolishly. Most certainly you are capable of being more than a castle clown. Should you except this apology of mine, using my gift of sorcery, I will bestow the good fortune onto you and your clan in becoming the ones who banish the great boar from these woods."

Now caught up in this charade and reflecting back on what I had learned in history class about the medieval ages, I decided to play along with this game by responding, "Although I find the idea of a beheading quite interesting, and might also consider the rack, tar and feathering, or perhaps a generous flogging, your apology is accepted as my show of mercy."

As this pair of oddballs ambled off, I asked Uncle Matt why he did not arrest them. Uncle Matt noted that as hunters, the impaired Renaissance actors were really no threat to anything in their condition. He did consider however, citing them for public intoxication. Uncle Matt then said that he found this duo more amusing than dangerous, and therefore, decided to let them simply head back to the Renaissance Faire. Still curious about these two costumed crusaders, I asked Uncle Matt what is a renaissance fair and the thing they called grog.

According to my uncle, Renaissance Fairs are a reenactment of English life during the times of Shakespeare, Queen Elizabeth, and King Henry VIII. These festivals involve people dressing up and performing as minstrels, magicians, acrobats, dancers, jugglers, jesters, crafters, merchants, knights, wizards, and crowned royalty. During these lively events, many of the participants consume a mixture of water and rum known as grog. This ale of sorts became a staple during the Middle Ages because it was safer to drink than plain water. Common to these fairs is a great feast featuring the roasting of a domestic pig. This menu item symbolizes the wild boars once hunted in past eras with crossbows, spears, and longbows.

Just on impulse, I had to ask my uncle, "Is grog anything like moonshine?" With a perplexed look, Uncle Matt answered, "Now that's a curious question. Both of them cause all kinds of trouble, yet, of the two, moonshine is much more potent. You would be smart not to sample either one." Knowing that a lot of the culprits dealt with by Uncle Matt and Ranger Walt, cause problems after hitting the bottle, I assured my uncle that based on his advice and stern lectures from Grandpa Nutter, there were no intentions on my part to become a boozer. Thinking to myself, I recalled Tustis's reference to liquor as bad medicine, Brother Oliver's story of how drinking almost ruined his life, and Sadie's notation that her Granpappy abstained from sipping any of his hooch and always refused selling to anyone whose consumption habits turned them into troublemakers. Most of all, I did not want to be anything like Boone, who always bragged about drinking and was dumb enough to smoke as well.

Turning to Ranger Walt, I then asked, "What made these two guys think they could find anything resembling a wild boar in this area?" To my surprise, this park ranger answered, "It's not entirely impossible. There have been reports over the years of several feral pigs spotted in the county north of here. Most likely, they are former domestic stock that have escaped some local farmer's pen and now are roaming about like wild boars. When this happens, these hogs take on shaggy coats of bristled hair and even grow nasty looking tusks, which they use to tear up farm crops and native roots to feed on. Weighing hundreds of pounds, they certainly can be menacing. Being prolific, a sow can produce up to three litters a year and thus establish a horde of havoc raising hogs."

Still surprised by this response, I once more asked, "But do you think there are any wild boars in these woods?" Ranger Walt then remarked, "Not that I know of, yet again, it is not completely impossible. As you well know, there are plenty of hiding places for unusual critters in this park. When walking about and exploring this place, you never quite know what or who you will run into! Now, isn't that so?"

Somehow it seemed that this park ranger's comments and ending question had a personal reference to me. His mentioning of what or who you might run into, suddenly made me feel as if my secret encounters in these woods were actually being witnessed. Did this ranger named Walt know about Sage? Was he familiar with Tustis, Brother Oliver, or Sadie? Were the dream pool, church window, and mineshaft known to him? And if any or all of this were true, would he tell Uncle Matt or anyone else of my woodland encounters?

While riding back to the park office in the ranger's jeep, I felt a terrible uneasiness within me. If word ever got around town that I had been meeting with Brother Oliver or Sadie, chances are I too would be talked about in the same gossiping ways that they continue to endure. Should it be mentioned I befriended a small wonder Indian, the questions would be endless. And worst of all, if it ever became revealed that I hang out with an owl, there is no telling what measures Boone and the other bullies would resort to.

After returning to the park office and climbing out of the jeep, Uncle Matt and I began walking toward the squad car. Before reaching the police vehicle, Ranger Walt called out to me. "Young man," he said, "Thank you for alerting us and helping to protect this park. It seems I now owe you a favor, which perhaps I can grant the next time we meet."

Just like Sadie had done when it came to our departure, Ranger Walt's parting words resembled more of a premonition than a farewell exchange. He seemed to know about something soon to come, that perhaps would involve me, and yet, to which I had no clue of what that could be. As if things had not already become complicated enough, another mysterious character now entered into my life.

# Wild Bill's Journal

---

*Pursuing new challenges means never leaving well enough alone.*

---

 oday promised to be like no other. In a hog wild encounter, brought together would be a wounded warrior, a small wonder man, an eccentric spinster, a jabbering owl, and of course, myself. In the midst of this haphazard rendezvous, a mysterious journal would reveal secrets connecting all of us.

Earlier this week, I celebrated my fourteenth birthday. As usual, Grandpa Nutter surprised me with something totally unanticipated. Walking from his bedroom, he carried with him a tattered looking old book. At first, I thought it was a timeworn bible. Tapping my imagination, I then sort of hoped that it might be an ancient wizard's book of spells and potions. "This is for your birthday," Grandpa said. "Handle it carefully, read it thoroughly, and never forget what it contains."

On a previous birthday, grandpa gave me a handful of lead musket balls. This was a personal treasure that he had acquired as a young kid. About five miles from here and near the river is an old smelting site known as the shot tower. It is where molten lead ore was dropped down a tall chimney-like structure and formed into rounded balls before descending into a cooling pool below. Supposedly, this operation produced and supplied many of the muzzleloader bullets used by the Union army during the Civil War. Grandpa Nutter's grandfather once worked at this shot tower, which is where these leads balls came from. It seems as if everything given to me by Grandpa Nutter has a history and local story behind it. This unusual book, now entrusted to me, would most likely be the same.

Upon opening the book's worn leather cover, I peered inside and could see that it was handwritten. Sensing my curiosity, Grandpa noted, "It's a journal and a special one at that. It belonged to a quirky old miser named William Lucas, who a couple of generations ago, lived not far from here. After being abandoned and sitting empty for several decades, this marooned homestead was purchased by Ranger Walt, who has done a pretty good job at restoring the place. In exchange for planting a grove of walnut seedlings on his property, Ranger Walt gave me this book. Because of my reputation as a local history buff, he thought this might be something I would appreciate. While remodeling the farmhouse, Ranger Walt discovered this book hidden inside one of the bedroom walls. As for Mr. Lucas, he was an accomplished artist and sketched the Native Americans who once lived in these parts. He was also a cantankerous old widower and hardcore drinker, referred to by most area folks as "Wild Bill. From all the time you spend exploring the woods around here, I figured you might enjoy this unusual book and its stories. Be careful, for it is a fragile old piece of local history."

Although the handwriting was sometimes difficult to read, I spent the rest of the week delving into this archaic journal. Throughout it, there were numerous sketches to match the writings. The more I read, the more intrigued I became. Like the dream pool which Tustis peered into, this journal suddenly opened up to me, secrets and stories. The most fascinating was a chapter titled "Farewell to Talon". By the time I finished this particular passage, my head was spinning with all kinds of questions. I now needed desperately to see Sage and gather together my other woodland friends.

For the next two days, it rained so hard, I could not leave the house. On the third day however, I packed the old journal into a rucksack and headed for Sage's den. Although this late summer day was sunny and warm, it seemed quite unusual. Unlike most days, when a few crows are mouthing off and numerous other birds are singing, no sounds could be heard. Nothing was stirring. There appeared to be a spell of silence cast upon the entire woods. The eerie quiet made me nervous. Looking around me, there were no signs of life and yet, I felt this sense of being watched. As such, my grip tightened on the hickory hiking stick.

Because of the soggy ground leftover from the recent storms, I had to trek carefully. Learning from the past, I was not about to take any misfortunate tumbles. Avoiding all potential hazards, I soon found myself approaching Sage's den. After traversing the hillside and peering up toward his home, I was surprised to see that Sage had company. Both Tustis and Brother Oliver were standing next to him. Facing one another, Tustis and Brother Oliver appeared to be conversing with sign language. Turning his gaze away from them and focusing on me, Sage exclaimed, "So, you have finally made it here!" In response I noted, "You sound as if you were expecting me." Replying in a scolding manner, sage retorted, "Yes, we have all been waiting for your arrival. First of all, there is something you should see right away and then afterwards, we must venture without haste to meet up with Sadie."

Feeling confused about this surprise reunion, I scratched my head and inquired, "What is going on?" Sage then stared at me and said, "Tustis has had two more visions. The first showed Tustis and Brother Oliver painting a new symbol on the wall of my den. In his second vision, all of us are sitting around a council fire. In this same vision, Tustis also saw you bringing to us what appears to be a book of some kind." Hearing this from Sage, I was now really puzzled. Tustis had already predicted my arrival and knew of the book I was carrying. Tustis had always amazed me, I was now in complete awe of this shaman.

Without getting a chance to contemplate this circumstance further, Sage signaled for me to follow him into his den. In doing so, not only did I again see the three symbols on the wall, yet, just opposite them was a newly painted marking. Somewhat startled, I now found myself peering at what seemed to be the drawing of an owl attacking a hog. Sensing my bewilderment about this new symbol, Sage interjected, "How do you like my newest décor? Under Tustis's guidance, Brother Oliver painted it this morning." Still bewildered, I responded back, "It certainly is interesting, yet I really do not understand it." Sage then answered, "As for now, none of us knows its meaning, yet Tustis assures me, that in short order, more will come to light."

Anxious to get going, Sage remarked, "Sadie has most likely reached the ridge of the Raggedy Oak by now and therefore, we must hurry on to meet with her." Based on my prior experiences with Sage, I knew better than to slow everything down by peppering this owl with any questions at this time. Not daring to dally, I obediently fell in line with this entourage and followed Sage eastward toward the ridge of the Raggedy Oak.

While marching along in single line formation, each of us remained silent. After completing about half the distance to our destination, a loud shriek sounded out in the woods. It seemed to come from the exact location we were heading, the ridge of the Raggedy Oak. Picking up the pace, Sage darted forward at a speed, much faster than anything I thought possible by this bird. The rest of us were finding it difficult to keep up with the accelerating owl.

As we dashed onward, the screams turned into words and I then began recognizing a familiar voice yelling out, "Go away you devil. Go away!" Drawing closer to the Raggedy Oak, another sound got added to the landscape. It echoed like enraged snorting. When the Raggedy Oak finally started coming into view, the medley of noise came to a startling conclusion. Perched up high in the branches of the Raggedy Oak was Sadie. Her eyes were cast downward at the most unbelievable animal I had ever witnessed. It was a humungous wild boar. This berserk critter kept circling the tree and rooting away at the ground with its menacing tusks.

While Tustis, Brother Oliver, and I stood awestruck, Sage charged forward without hesitation. Using every ounce of strength in his body, he leaped into the air with his wings extended and talons fully exposed. As he descended downward, his claws pierced into the fat haunches of this grizzly looking hog. Squealing from pain and terror, the shocked swine bucked up and down like a bronco being busted. When Sage finally let go, the hog spun around and sprinted off across the ridge. Without ever looking back, the panicked pig then quickly disappeared. At the speed this critter was retreating, it would be only a matter of minutes before he exited the park and headed for another county.

Climbing down from her perch in the Raggedy Oak, Sadie, even though visibly shaken, began showcasing a huge grin and said to Sage, "Looks like you arrived just in the nick of time. Never in my life have I ever experienced a cantankerous critter like that. From the lashing you gave him, hopefully that porker won't venture into these parts again."

Still stunned by this escapade, I began thinking back about the previous confrontation with the two Renaissance men. Although seeming outlandish and odd, their warnings about a wild boar rang true. Now also just as genuine was the prophecy symbolized on the wall of the old mine shaft. And even though these predictions had at last come to light,, it baffled me considerably that a renegade wild boar had entered my realm. Its appearance and departure not only added to the magic and mystery of these woods, yet created a newfound element of danger.

As we all finally calmed down and gathered together near the Raggedy Oak, Tustis looked to Sage and proclaimed, "You are indeed the bravest among us." In response, Sage then retorted, "Whenever my feathers get ruffled, I just do what I've got to do. And I must say, that was quite exciting, wasn't it? However, we now have other business at hand. Vandy, is there something you wish to show us?"

With everyone now staring at me, I bashfully froze as I often do. Recognizing my dilemma, Sage broke the silence by stating, "We are more than curious about what you have brought to us in that rucksack." While I began removing the book, Tustis spoke up and said, "This is a time for council. Therefore, we must first build a council fire to gather around." Scurrying about, everyone began fetching twigs and branches for a small bonfire. As the fire got ignited and flames danced, I nervously thought about all the fire restrictions that exist in this park. I then desperately prayed that the quickly rising smoke would not catch anyone else's attention.

After instructing all of us to be seated in a circle around this fire, Tustis turned to me and said, "My visions noted that there is something in that book which you must share at this gathering." Still nervous about now being the center of attention, I mustered some composure and responded back, "This book given to me by my grandfather has a special chapter in it. If possible and because I am too nervous to do it myself, I would like Brother Oliver to read this chapter to everyone here." With this said, Tustis lifted his hands and began signing my wish to Brother Oliver. Reaching out to me, the brown robed monk accepted the book, which I had opened to the chapter titled, *Farewell to Talon*. As this makeshift council sat in anticipation, a soft and deep voice recited the following, as written by Wild Bill;

"Today is perhaps the second saddest day of my life. The only one with more suffering was that time when I failed to rescue my dear wife Edna from drowning in the nearby river. Just after the dawn of this morning, several Indian braves approached my homestead. They came bearing news that my closest friend, Talon had passed on to the Great Spirit. Although known to me that the last of his days had been near, I grieved deeply for this cherished comrade and honorable man. My only means of coping now with this loss is to script one of the strangest episodes in both our lives.

It was almost two decades ago when at the start of summer, a strange man dressed in a top hat and suit, set up camp just down the road. He claimed to be an agent of the Ringling Brothers Circus, whose home base was 20 miles north of here. According to the sign posted in his camp, this stranger was recruiting for giants, midgets, bearded ladies, overly fat fellows, disfigured men, tattooed people, fire eaters, sword swallowers, and all other oddities interested in circus work. At the bottom of his sign was a $500 bounty being offered for live capture of the "Elf Indian". When he initially stopped by my place and asked to set up his camp in my meadow, I told him I wanted no part of such skullduggery business and sent him on his way. Unfortunately, my neighbor to the south was more accommodating and that is where he set up camp.

As word got out about the Elf Indian bounty, every local scoundrel began scouring the area woods. This of course included the Dank brothers, Willis, Clyde, Lyle, and their cousin Cade. Twice I had to kick them off my property and threaten to fetch the sheriff. I had ongoing run-ins with this clan of hooligan hillbillies. They have stolen chickens from me, raided my garden, started a fire near my apple orchard, and hijacked a jug of hooch. These varmints are so low, they would turn in their own grandmother if a bounty was posted.

No sooner had I run the Dank brothers off my land when the strangest of strangers came wandering about. His name was Cyrus Loone and boasted of being the best of bounty hunters. He bragged that if need be, his hound could even follow the scent of a ghost. This weird character dressed as if he had stepped out of the distant past. His clothes, hat, and shoes were those of buckskin pioneer days. He carried with him both an old muzzleloader rifle and powder horn. Wirey in frame and sporting a devilish pointed nose, Cyrus Loone created a sense of deviance about him. As with the Dank brothers, I escorted Mr. Loone from my land and told him sternly that I would have no part in any manhunt. Mr. Loone then sneered at me and responded, "Perhaps and perhaps not, yet you will not stop me from prevailing at what I do best." He then spit on the ground and ventured off without looking back. Not trusting this varmint, I strongly suspected his return.

Just when I thought I was through running folks off my land, Henry Horn came driving in on his buckboard. This actually was welcome news, because I was almost out of moonshine and right about now, really needed a good swallow of Henry's bottled satisfaction. To my surprise however, instead of several jugs in the back of his wagon, Henry appeared to be bringing me an entire barrel.

No sooner had Henry jumped off his wagon, then he began calling out to me. "Remember that money you owe me for past deliveries?" Henry asked. "I am about to give you a proposition to get rid of that debt." Henry then walked to the back of his wagon, pointed to the barrel, and remarked, "If you are willing to store this barrel and hide its content for several weeks, I'll call us even."

Being a shrewd moonshining businessman, Henry was not the kind to write off debts so easily. Even though I trusted him as a long time associate, there had to be a catch. "You sure must have some kind of special hooch in order to offer me such terms." I said. Henry quickly replied, "That I truly do. Climb on up and I'll show you." Following Henry, I then moved toward the barrel. Henry grabbed a pry bar and began propping the top off this barrel. Before I even had the chance to look inside, I got shocked by the sight of the little man crawling out. From his size and attire, I knew instantly who this was. "Holy Moses!" I said. "The entire county is searching for this Indian." "I know," said Henry. "For almost a week now, he has stowed away in one of my old mine shafts. However, as a good friend to both of us, Talon deserves better accommodations. As such, we need to help him out. Being as ornery as you are, I reckon your place to be the best hideout. And besides, you do owe me!" Henry then walked to the front of his buckboard, retrieved two jugs, and exclaimed, "Perhaps this will help to seal the deal!"

Due to the fact that there are a lot of old buildings on my property and for various reasons most folks are afraid of visiting me, it did make sense for Talon to hide out here in the meantime. Because I did not want to jeopardize any more hooch deliveries and actually owed Talon a favor as well, I agreed to help out. With that, Talon took up residence in my old granary.

Years ago, I had met Talon while visiting his family's village. For quite some time I had been wanting to sketch pictures of his people. In order to do so, I needed the blessing of their shaman. That shaman of course was Talon. Following a number of visits and ceremonies, Talon proclaimed me a brother and granted permission for my artwork. According to Talon, he had a vision that my sketches would preserve the memories of his people. Talon also noted that by allowing me to do this artwork would require a favor in return. I guess that favor was now being called upon.

During this time with Talon, he shared with me tales of the local tribal nations. He talked about the courage of Black Hawk and other Native American chiefs while dealing with broken treaties and skirmishes over land claims. Talon also noted the long history of shamans within his family and the short members born every other generation. They became revered and referred to as "Sageawah", a word meaning small wonder.

About two weeks into his hiding out at my place, both Talon and I were getting restless about his confinement. It was then I began noticing a return by the Dank brothers along the east boundaries of my land. At the same time, Cyrus Loone again skulked along the western border. Obviously in cahoots with each other, both parties were getting to close for comfort. Something needed to be done. I handed Talon an old Colt six shooter and told him to remain in the granary. I next grabbed my trusty double-barreled .12 gauge and walked about fifty yards east of my house.

Raising the shotgun to my shoulder, I pointed skyward and fired. As the echoes of the blast diminished, I then hollered out, "The next one is for you Dank brothers." I then turned around and walked westward toward the ridge which Cyrus Loone was on. Again, I lifted the gun and fired upward. "I have got one for you as well Loone." All of a sudden, several figures carrying rifles came running down my road. It was Sheriff Morey and his deputies. "What in tarnation is going on?" yelled Sheriff Morey. In response, I glanced at the sheriff and noted, "Just enforcing some trespassing laws." With a look of frustration, the sheriff replied. "I know all about that. I've had ongoing complaints for weeks about cockeyed bounty hunters. Quite frankly, nobody is going to hunt down anyone in my county, especially when that someone has done nothing criminal. I just got through booting that circus agent out of these parts. With your permission, I'll take care of these remaining trespassers as well.

Sheriff Morey is notorious for chasing scoundrels out of this county. He especially despises the gypsies who wander through here twice a year. Any local resident seeing the approach of a brightly painted wagon would hurry to lock up their smokehouses, chicken coops, and homes. Even the gardens have to be closely guarded against these intruders, who most locals call beggars and swipers. There were claims that the gypsies would place curses on anyone who refused to feed them and even resort to kidnapping children.

At first, some thought that perhaps the so called "circus agent" was nothing more than a conniving gypsy. Eventually, it got discovered that this stranger did not represent the Ringling Brothers after all. He had been recently fired by them and intended to start his own carnival sideshows. This swindler also did not have any of the funds intended to pay a bounty.

Most folks around here do not want to mess with Sheriff Morey. Some claim he is even more cantankerous than even me. Besides, he is married to a woman who is part Indian and quite protective of the sparse tribal members still in this region. Because of his connections to several politicians and the current Governor, Sheriff Morey is pretty much the law of the land. It is even well-known that Henry Horn's bootlegging is preserved and guarded by this local sheriff.

It did not take long for the sheriff and his deputies to run the Dank Brothers and Cyrus Loone off my land. After just a matter of days, everything was back to normal. The bounty hunters were gone for good. Circus agents never again set up shop in this county. And as for Talon, he returned to his spiritual practices and pursuits. Amongst the local folklore, tales continued about an Elf Indian and his magical powers.

With his passing, I must now rely on memories rather than conversations. His gift to me of an owl-faced dream catcher will now serve as a memorial in my home. I am really going to miss this friend of mine. Talon was one of the few that could tolerate me. He became my healer during hard times and helped me to overcome the loss of my dear wife, Edna. This shaman taught me so much about the heritage of his people. And what I will miss most of all are his fascinating stories. Foreseen in his visions, Talon believed that upon his passing into another life, his spirit will eventually return to this world and be carried within a mysterious creature bearing great wisdom. Talon then claimed that this figure would be joined by others, who together, will create a rebirth for the Clan of the Owl. And in union, these members will forever preserve memories of the past. Always intrigued by this magnificent man, I know better than to doubt any of his predictions. Oftentimes in my own dreams, I also see my traditions being continued by another family artist. Perhaps, somewhere and somehow, Talon and I will both be remembered."

As this journal chapter came to a close, Brother Oliver paused momentarily while reflecting on what he had just read. Like all of us within this council circle, he appeared lost in thought about Wild Bill's writings. Turning his head from side to side and glancing at each of us, Brother Oliver then said, "What I have just read indeed has special meaning to all of us here. There is something more which I personally need to share with you. At the end of each chapter in this journal is what appears to be the word OWL. However, based on my family's history, I know this to be a signature representing three initials. They belong to a man named Oliver William Lucas, my great, great grandfather and namesake. As such, Wild Bill and I are kindred spirits.

Pausing once again, Brother Oliver turned his eyes toward Tustis. Given this cue, Tustis then spoke out, "This revelation of your ancestor is equally shared by me, for it is my grandfather Talon, who is revealed in this story as well. And of course, Sadie, it was your grandfather Henry who helped to create the bond between our ancestors."

Now given her turn to speak, Sadie teared up a bit while saying, "Granpappy Henry always talked so fondly of Talon and Bill. However, there is yet another kinship connection within the story we have just heard. The sheriff called Morey was a nickname for a man whose family name was Elmore Christianson." With this stated, Sadie then focused on me and pronounced, "Therefore Vandy, Sheriff Morey was the grandfather to your grandfather!"

Being so much younger than all those now around me and dumbfounded by all the revelations, I didn't know how to respond at this time. As usual, Sage came to my rescue by interjecting, "It seems that not only are all of us connected by being otherwise, yet also through past histories and kinships. I know that we sometimes feel like loners and misfits, yet as of today however, each member is one someone and a part of everybody in this revived Clan of the Owl."

As Sage ended his speech, approaching footsteps could be heard from below the ridge. Peering down into the valley, we could now see that two men were climbing up the hillside. Moments later, I recognized this duo as Grandpa Nutter and Ranger Walt. As he approached our council circle, Grandpa hollered out, "Looks like you've prepared a fire big enough to roast a hog." Following up, Ranger Walt then remarked, "Of course, based on what I saw today of that wild hog racing past the ranger station, he'll never be caught for any such feast. And by the way, if you douse that fire properly, I'll overlook those smoke signals you sent to us."

Upon joining into our circle, Grandpa Nutter explained how he had sighted the smoke billowing from the woods and immediately contacted

Ranger Walt. After hearing from Walt about the hog sighting, Grandpa Nutter and the park ranger both speculated that something out of the ordinary was afoot in the forest. Spotting the journal still being held by Brother Oliver, Grandpa noted, "Seeing that book again and based on what I have read from it, there is no doubt on my part what this is all about. Having gotten that journal from Ranger Walt, I'm pretty sure he knows all about this as well."

In response, Ranger Walt cast a look at each of us and said, "Since discovering Wild Bill's journal a few years back, I've kept a careful eye on these woods. In doing so, I have also watched each of you crossing paths and becoming connected. Though I cannot allow any more council fires, I'll keep sentry over these woods so that your clan continues to discover the secrets and mysteries of this place. However, it will be up to each of you as to what can be revealed and to whom it can be shared."

As this strange coalition remained gathered on this day, both Tustis and Grandpa Nutter took it upon themselves to endow us with their storytelling skills. When it finally became time to disband, it was decided that Brother Oliver should keep in his possession the journal of Wild Bill. With the fire thoroughly doused, there seemed to be a vow of silence as each of us headed off in varying directions. Walking side by side with Grandpa Nutter, this silence remained as we contemplated the day's events. Neither Grandpa Nutter nor I could find the right words to explain how we felt. It had become obvious to me that my grandfather knew all along about the reasons for my treks into the woods and the secrets I had discovered. It had also become obvious in the council circle, that Grandpa Nutter was well-acquainted with everyone there.

As I tossed in bed on this evening and tried to piece together the events of this day, it kept occurring to me all that I had learned from both Grandpa Nutter and Sage. Because both had spent so much time in these nearby woods, it became hard for me to decide which one of them was the wisest critter in the forest. Now finding out that Grandpa Nutter was part Native American, perhaps it was within him that Talon's spirit lives on. However, there is no denying that an earth owl with a bum wing and gift for gab embodies this same spirit, which is like no other and most definitely otherwise.

Within this rebirthed Clan of the Owl, I now have a circle of extraordinary friends, who are leading me not only to new discoveries, but also teaching me that in other words and other ways, it's absolutely okay to be otherwise. And so, I will be just that.

######### *The End* #########

# Some Added tale FEATHERs

*evelations from the Author:* When a story is written and labeled a fantasy fiction, there is an assumption that everything is make-believe. Nothing could be farther from the truth in Bum Wing. Although whimsically embellished, the setting is based on a very real place and the characters patterned after some of the locals who reside here. As for some of the adventures noted in this story, many are similar to those which I experienced as a young whippersnapper.

Within my homeland of southwestern Wisconsin, there is a vast woodland christened Governor Dodge State Park. It lies in the uplands between two small burghs called Dodgeville and Spring Green. Rather than being a backyard, this park represented an extension of the front yard to my country home. Just by crossing the road, I got to spend many of my youth years exploring this place of zombie trees, treasure troves, and clandestine critters. To the best of my knowledge, many still exist.

Dubbed the "Driftless" area, by no means is this region anything of the ordinary. It got bypassed by the receding glaciers of the Ice Age, and as a result, became landmarked as a highlands of rocky bluffs, twisting waterways, and hidden ravines. Since the mid-1800's, miners and other early settlers began telling tales of the spirits which they claimed, inhabited and haunted these places. These early day immigrants also told of the bison, elk, and bears which once roamed about this region in great numbers. There would be stories as well about an evolution of this area that began with mining, progressed onto logging, turned to harvesting wheat and tobacco and eventually became a stronghold for dairy farming. And finally there are those fortunate ones who could recollect about surviving local epidemics of cholera, measles, tuberculosis, and flu. As such, this homeland has indeed seen its share of changes.

To get to this region and the park, you need to roll along Highway 23. Travelling from the north, you will meander through Wyoming Valley, climb a winding grade which some call Van's Hill, and pass by Percussion Rock Road. Farther on down the road is Deer Shelter Rock, known nowadays as the famous House on the Rock. Journeying from the south on this same highway, a now horseless "George of all trades" homestead will eventually come into view. Behind it remains the Old Rock Church. Because of the spooky nature of this chapel site, a production crew from California ventured here and filmed a horror flick a few years back. If inclined to stop at this country church, you will find that not only is "Big O" George Slaney buried here in its quaint cemetery, yet also my great grandfather Christianson and other Norwegian ancestors. Hidden away in area barns, George's collection of horse drawn relics still remain intact. On his family's property is one of the park's pioneer farm buildings which George moved during an excavation. If I am not mistaken, this is the same barn which almost decapitated my head when George attempted to teach me how to ride one of his horses. This experience of course is coincidentally similar to that of Vandy's first vamoose on a horse. And by the way, George really owned a massive rodeo bull named Caesar.

Venturing into the state park, there are trail signs directing you to Enee Point, Thomas' Cave, and Stephens' Falls. However, in order to find the other waterfalls and the dream pool that will require a vision quest by backtracking from Cox Hollow Lake and following the small spring which represents its headwaters. Along the ridge above this waterfall, the remnants of the heirloom apple orchard continue to blossom. A few Oakists may dwell there as well.

Although once regarded as snake country, this distinction no longer exists. According to the county archives, waves of rattlesnakes would appear around here whenever heavy rainstorms flushed them out of their dens. In order to remedy this problem, the county posted a bounty for each rattler rounded up, dead or alive. This process pretty much wiped out the viper population. Despite all my sojourns into this park, I have yet to encounter any timber rattlers. However, many of the locals, especially the old timers, can tell you about all the rattlesnakes Woody Roberts captured in this region. As such, it is best to poke about the rock crevices and dens with a trusty hickory stick rather than an arm or leg.

As far as I know, the old Model T still remains hidden in a ravine just off the Lost Canyon trail. Exposed to the elements, its body and framework have become woodpeckered by years of rusting. In some of the nearby gullies, many of the pioneer dumpsites are buried within the weed patches. They contain, or at least use to, all the intriguing items noted by Vandy. Again, due to rusting, the true identities of these vintage cast-offs have now weathered away.

Even though many of the aging zombie trees and raggedy oaks have fallen into decay, there are constantly replacements taking root throughout the ridges and valleys. Search thoroughly and you will eventually encounter a misshapen and ominous Oakist. Upon spotting any with hollow cavities, be ever so cautious of poking your nose into these shadowy enclaves and coming face to face with a pair of eyes staring back. It has happened to me more than once.

Two lakes now grace these woodlands, Cox Hollow and Twin Valley. However the hidden Halverson Ponds are sadly and forever gone. Based on local legend, there used to be a long ago mink ranch near these ponds. At the far eastern end of Twin Valley Lake, turkey vultures soar about in their eerie manner. Just as spooky are the sea monsters of this particular lake. Known as Muskies, these toothy underwater leviathans skulk about in the murky depths and possess the potential to viciously attack swimmers. These scaly denizens can often exceed four feet in length. Those too wimpy to deal with the muskies, often choose Cox Hollow Lake instead, where the only menaces are the giant bullheads.

According to my sister Kathy, this park and the region around it remain haunted by the Ridgeway Phantom. Stories and sightings of this homegrown ghost date back to the pioneer days. Her heritage Polkinghorn farm receives regular visits from specters of this sort. These sinister spirits can easily reside and hide in the dense nearby wooded hollows or dark twisted underworlds of the old lead ore mines.

Should there be any curiosity relating to wild boars in this area, reports from the neighboring county, north of here, claim that grizzly looking feral hogs are pillaging and plundering the farmlands. At the same time, frequent sightings have been reported of a misguided marauding cougar.

Oddly enough, a red kangaroo on the loose, romped around here not long ago. It is even possible that an escaped emu from a failed local ranch operation might still be lurking about.

While trekking through the area's woods, do not be reckless enough to push over any old stumps. When I last did so, a critter really did rumble and tumble out. Instead of being feathered, this guy was furry, masked, ring-tailed, and snarling. Without a doubt, he was truly more than miffed about the situation. To this day, I still feel bad about being the one who made him homeless.

If wondering about the morel and ginseng patches sought out by Sadie. They do exist in this neck of the woods. However, you are on your own to find them. And should you want to be told on how to locate that old mine shaft where a wise old owl resides, unlike Sage, I am not talking.

When wandering south of the park and into my Dodgeville hometown, don't be surprised to find many of the sites noted in this book. Harry's horse barn is still there, as is the historic courthouse, slag furnace, and a plague cemetery where over one hundred victims of a cholera epidemic were laid to rest. This is a place where Sadie's parents might have been buried. Twisting about town is an underground network of forlorn mineshafts. During my dad's generation, kids would sneak into these mines to explore them.

Two real-life resident giants mark this town's past. The Scotch Giant indeed served as an international headliner for P.T. Barnum's Circus. The second formidable figure donned a police uniform. Patrolling about years ago was an enormous policeman named Merle Carroll. Fondly referred to as Officer Tiny, he tipped the scales at 407 pounds. Just when I thought that Officer Tiny could perhaps be the most gargantuan cop of all time, I recently discovered that during the early 1900's, a seven and a half foot giant christened "Big Gust" served as Marshall and lamplighter in a small town north of here.

Another authentic and eccentric character was a man named Archibald McArthur, who got labeled the Dodgeville Hermit. During the late 1800's, the long-bearded Archibald completely abandoned his attorney practice and shied away from society. On a daily basis, he began loitering in the East Side Cemetery and communing with the spirits. In some ways, Brother Oliver is patterned after this reclusive character of the town's past. Brother Oliver's religious persona also copies that of a kooky local merchant who dressed as a monk while hawking curiosities at an area flea market. Attired in a long hooded brown robe and crowned by a thin ring of hair encircling his bald scalp, no one seems to be quite sure as to whether this guy actually had any ministerial ties.

In further regards to the character of Brother Oliver, he is quite typical of many Vietnam era veterans, who upon returning from this unpopular war of twenty years, were greeted with scrutiny. Rather than being rightfully honored, these vets became the targets of political protests and media bashing. Over 50,000 of their fellow U.S. servicemen died during this war. Those who survived often carried with them lifelong battle scars and wounds. Some even felt a sense of guilt for not perishing alongside their buddies. It was not until the Vietnam War Memorial got constructed, that this country finally began to realize the service and sacrifices of these veterans.

In every town there is a quirky old maid or two. Sadie mimics one of the spinster sisters from an eccentric duo called the Bushkees. These sauntering siblings lived in an old miner's cabin near the eastern outskirts of Dodgeville and were often the subject of local gossip. Most everyone in this town knew of them, yet very few actually knew anything about these mysterious ladies. As such, these gals gained an incredible notoriety due to exaggerated tales of their shadowy appearances, ramshackle home, and daffy behavior.

Sadie's character also mocks that of an elderly widower named George Tyre. This eccentric loner lived on the southeast side of town and foraged about in a shadowy area known as Black's Grove. While armed with either a squirrel gun or an ax, this picker often exited Black's Grove carrying items scrounged from the smoldering town dump. George's property became a testament to all the salvaged cast-offs recovered by him. Similar to Sadie, his self-dependent and reclusive nature led to a fair amount of wonderment about this local geezer.

The Snipe hunt trickery referred to by Brother Oliver is a long time rural tradition. Generally, this spoof is used by country folks needing to put know-it-all city slickers in their place. Snipe really do exist, however, these funny looking marsh birds with stilt legs and Pinocchio beaks are not prone to frequenting any woods. Capturing one with nothing more than a gunny sack, would be quite the fete.

Wild Bill's tale of the hunt for the Elf Indian is not far from what could have been a true occurrence. During the late 19th and early 20th centuries, circus shows were rampant in this part of the country. These were fiercely competitive businesses vying for the attention of audiences in any way they could. To this end, freak shows became an incredible draw. As previously noted, this included a local connection known as the Scotch Giant. There is nothing make-believe about this local farmer and teamster who stood at 7 foot two inches, and weighed 340 pounds. In reality, he was a Cornish immigrant named Frederick Shadick, whose wife Jane Gray, towered as well at seven feet tall. Back in the late 1800's, this enormous man became a spectacle as he drove ore carts, back and forth along Highway 23. As a result of his monumental reputation, Mr. Shadick got tracked down by P.T. Barnum to star in his circus freak show. Frederick teamed up with a miniature man named General Tom Thumb and instantly became a worldwide sensation. An old circus poster showcases this goliath lifting a Shetland pony above his head. Because of his celebrity status and worldwide travels, the Scotch Giant even got accused as being party to a spy conspiracy and several murder plots. He died suddenly at age 47 from what some called suspicious poisoning.

Freak shows thrived on exploiting the odd, outlandish, and ugly aspects of humanity. Any persons with grotesque abnormalities or unusual sizes were coveted as headliners. At the tail end of the freak show era, I still remember seeing the Lobster Boy with his huge claw hands, the Alligator Lady with her leathery reptile skin, and a guy called Popeye, whose left eye would pop out of the socket and dangle about for a gawking audience.

Although freak shows have fortunately diminished, in their heyday, someone such as a small wonder Indian would have been readily sought after. The creation of the Tustis character, and Talon as well, serves as a complete opposite to the Scotch Giant. Part of the lore, relating to this Native American, stems from a local legend of the Hiding Kickapoo. Several decades ago, a lone American Indian man was routinely spotted in native garb and roaming the region. Despite search parties discovering his nomadic dwelling places, no one was ever able to track down this mysterious nomad.

In Native American lore, tribes such as the Cherokee and Iroquois make reference to clans of "Little People" among them. Some of their legends venerate these Little People as having special religious significance, while other stories tell of their prowess as arrow makers. As a shaman, Tustis would be revered as a healer, historian, naturalist, and spiritual leader.

The name given to the small wonder shaman in this book, honors my friend Darwin Simtustis, a Native American who grew up in the wild West on the Warm Springs Reservation. Darwin taught me many things about his proud and storied culture.

In some ways similar to Tustis, Wild Bill represented a shaman of sorts. His stint as a water witch was a common practice utilized by many pioneer farmers searching for wells to dig. Even some of the lead and zinc miners claimed the ability to locate ore deposits through the use of a forked dousing stick. Gifted individuals like Wild Bill, just had a knack for finding underground waterways.

In a different type of quest for liquidity, there was another practice more common than water witch dousing. Anytime you dig into the past of a hometown, you are more than likely to discover that a moonshining operation existed. Just a block behind my paternal grandfather's home on the southern end of Iowa street, a enterprising man named Stanley Trench set up a local moonshining business. Inside a small barn on the property was a full-fledged still and horse stable. Just like Henry Horn, Mr. Trench flourished as a bootlegger in a town designated dry and liquor free. A good portion of his hooch ended up at a speak-easy within the Higbee Hotel. My dad admitted to assisting Mr. Trench with deliveries to a social establishment, just outside the city limits. It was also purported that Mr. Trench's distilled spirits were kept behind the counter at the corner drug store and made available for medicinal purposes. Some of this bottled corn mash might still be buried within the sealed up root cellar that once existed between my grandfather's home and Mr. Trench's property.

Although the two Renaissance characters might seem a bit far-fetched, small hometowns like mine, have never been strangers to strangers. The first half of the 20th century represented an era of vagabonds such as gypsies and hobos. Traveling from one rural town to the next, these drifters were more often shunned than welcomed. In my community, a rail yard area known as Dirty Hollow hosted a hobo encampment. My grandmother Anderson use to guard the chicken coop whenever a tramp got spotted wandering the railroad that bordered her farm. And if any claimed to be a traveling salesman, the farmers were quick to hide and safeguard their daughters.

As a reoccurring character in Bum Wing, Grandpa Nutter is based on a combination of two old timers in my life. They include my storytelling maternal grandfather, Tom Anderson, and fishing buddy, Reuben Forseth. However, there is no connection by either one to collecting or planting nuts. Grandpa Tom labored as a pioneer farmer, who cleared the land and busted sod to create a dairy farm. Not only did he teach me to respect the land and study the seasons, yet his homestead also created hayloft, corn crib, and silo climbing adventures. My time among his spotted Holsteins, squealing pigs, wooly sheep, cackling chickens, barnyard cats, and an occasional coon dog, taught me lessons as well about the lives of critters.

My relationship with Reuben took me in many directions, most of which were toward favorite fishing holes. The two of us became acquainted with every twist and turn of Mill Creek. During our days of sitting on the banks of the Wisconsin River, I got to witness an ever changing waterway of sand bars, ominous eddies, deep channels, and treacherous currents. Together, Reuben and I battled the watery weirdos of this river which included mudcats, dogffish, sheepsheads, longnose gars, shovelnose sturgeons, and redhorses. Considering the creepy creatures lurking in these area waters, it is not hard to imagine what else might stalk about in the bordering marshes and woodlands.

Grandpa Tom and Reuben were just a few of the numerous elders who influenced my life. Perhaps that is why so many of the characters in Bum Wing are wise old owls, just like Sage. However, I have yet to say much about the youngest figure in this book.

Vandy's antics are true depictions of what kids did in the 1950's & 60's. These shenanigans included attaching baseball or playing cards to bicycle spokes, collecting cereal box posters, mailing in box tops and labels for prizes, coveting metal lunchboxes with favorite character and show themes, and battling in playground games of Red Rover and Pom Pom Pullaway. Watching an overload of westerns really was the craze. Even the Saturday morning cartoons got caught up in this trend with Quick Draw McGraw, Ricochet Rabbit & Droop-a-Long, Deputy Dawg, and Yosemite Sam.

In Dodgeville, pedaling treks to Brennan's Bridge and the Culvert were actual adventures. Chocolate milk hangovers resulted during June Dairy Days. Just about every family making an excursion to the Wisconsin Dells, returned with a genuine American Indian souvenir, some of which showcased a stamp stating "Made in China". Many of the local kids did really learn to ride at Harry Dowling's horse barn. And indeed, all of us got bewitched and bewildered by the notorious Bushkee sisters.

In closing, I have this to mention about Vandy. Every hometown has its Charlie Browns. He or she is that young kid continually striving to somehow fit in. In other words and other ways, the whole idea is to adapt when being otherwise. Doing so is not always easy, yet it can be accomplished with a fair share of initiative, a bit of confidence, and a little help from some friends.

Finally, in reference to the existence of talking owls, let's just keep in mind, that regardless of fact or fiction, magical and mystical things really do take place among the critters and characters within any woods. And no matter whether these woods border your yard, occur in a distant land, or simply represent a patch of trees just down the road, what exists within them is only limited by your own imagination.

# TEACHERS GUIDE: Questions for discussions in the classroom

Bum Wing is not only a book of adventures, yet it also represents a story about adversity and real issues. The following are suggestions for classroom discussions:

## BEING OTHERWISE:

Although Vandy and his circle of friends distinguished themselves as being otherwise, each had to overcome adversity and establish individual identities before coming together.

*Why are some people looked upon and treated as different? What kind of obstacles and barriers do they have to deal with? How can these challenges turn into inspirations and achievements? What did Talon mean when he said, "Those who are less than perfect are more than gifted?"*

## FIRST NATION ROOTS:

Tustis represents a First Nation heritage. Our American history did not begin when European settlers started immigrating to this country. The deep-rooted culture of this land got initially cultivated by its Native American people.

*Which tribal nations resided in this region? What was unique to their culture and heritage? Where are these people now?*

## REMEMBERING OUR VETERANS:

By serving his country, Brother Oliver shaped history and preserved freedoms. Like far too many veterans, his patriotic services became forgotten.

*Who are the military veterans in this community? What part of American history do they represent? How are they being remembered?*

## GROWING LONG IN THE TOOTH:

Sadie would not be an unusual character in most communities. Living alone and struggling to be independent, her situation is one which often gets ignored and overlooked. Nonetheless, she somehow survives as one of our neighbors.

*Are their folks like Sadie living in this community? How is it that they become alone and sometimes isolated? What is their role among us?*

## DRIFTING AWAY FROM THE DRIFTERS:

Strangers stick out like sore thumbs in small communities. As such, the flamboyant gypsies and ragamuffin hobos oftentimes became spectacles, wherever they wandered. The same applied to traveling circuses with their freak shows.

*What became of the gypsies and hobos from yesteryears? Do any still roam about? Did a hobo encampment ever exist in this community? What became of circus freak shows?*

## RELATIVELY SPEAKING:

Grandpa Nutter, Granpappy Henry, Talon, Wild Bill, and Sheriff Morey were each connected to Bum Wing characters as grandfathers, great grandfathers, and even great, great grandfathers. When tracing the genealogy of any family or community, a network of related connections becomes revealed.

*Have you ever traced your family tree? Are there any characters of special interest in your family's past? How does one go about researching genealogy?*

## GIVE A HOOT:

Although Sage is one of a kind, there are varying owls which inhabit just about every region. Though occasionally heard and seldom seen, they are secretive critters. However, most of us would be surprised by the assortment of owls hooting about in any neck of the woods.

*What owls are common in this region? Are they only creatures of the night? How do you go about finding an owl? Why are owls considered to be ever so wise?*

## SOBERING HERITAGE:

There indeed was a time when many communities had hometown moonshiners, bootleggers, speakeasies, and nip joints. These same communities were also influenced by prohibition and the temperance movement.

*Were these intoxicating traditions ever a part of this community's history? What made them so popular back in times past? How have perceptions about these traditions changed today?*

# QUIZING YOUR OWLISH WISDOM

As primarily creatures of the night, owls are often associated with myths about darkness and sorcery. Because of their secretive nature and eerie cries, these unique feathered critters have become main characters in fables and folklore. Here are some of the most common questions about owls.

*How many kinds of owls are there?*

> Scientists believe there are almost 155 species of owls. In North America, 19 different kinds of owls can be found.

*How far back do the oldest owl fossils date?*

> As a group of birds, owls have been around for 70 to 80 million years.

*Why do owls hoot?*

> Although owls can call out in many ways, not all of them hoot. Those that do, give a hoot as a territorial warning for others to stay away or use this sound to communicate to their young, and attract mates.

*How far around can an owl turn its head?*

> An owl can turn its head as much as 270 degrees.

*What do you call a grouping of owls?*

> Unlike some other birds which congregate in flocks, coveys, and gaggles, the most common term for a group of owls is a parliament. However, other terms have sometimes been used such as bazaar, brood, congress, state, glaring, stooping, wisdom, and hooting of owls.

*What do you call a baby owl?*

> A baby owl is called an owlet.

*Which is the largest of owls?*

Being more common, most think of the Great Horned Owl as the largest of owls. Also considered might be the Snowy Owl. However, in terms of length and weight, both the Eagle Owl and Great Gray Owl are larger.

*Which is the smallest of owls?*

The most pint-size of owls would be the Pygmy Owl and the even slightly smaller Elf Owl.

*What would be the widest of wingspans for an owl?*

A female Eagle owl can have a wingspan topping seven feet.

*What do owls eat?*

Generally, owls eat rodents, small mammals, insects, and other birds, whereas a few species favor fish and amphibians. There are some who claim that owls are one of the few predators daring to attack and devour a skunk.

*Can an owl be kept as a pet?*

Laws relating to the ownership of owls vary from country to country. In both the United States and Australia, it is illegal to keep an owl as a pet. The only exceptions are wildlife caretakers with rehabilitation licenses.

*Which is the only continent not home to any owls?*

No owls reside in Antarctica.

# About the Author

s an artist and folk-tattling author in the Wisconsin northwoods, D.S. Sully intertwines reality, fantasy, and mystery. Embellished with whimsical fact and fiction, his tales reflect the misadventures of everyday life. And while doing so, these same stories echo the exploits that he oftentimes experienced as a small town kid venturing beyond the outskirts.

D.S. Sully founded the *Write Ability Workshop*, a forum to teach adults and children facing challenges, how to script their life's experiences. He also hosts the *Give a Hoot Project*, involving visits to schools, libraries, children's hospitals, zoos, wildlife centers, and family events. The author is a member with the Society of Children's Book Writers & Illustrators. To contact D.S. Sully about his writings or activities, you can do so through the publisher at: **authorsupport@authorhouse.com**

# Other Books by D.S. Sully

*THE FLICKERING* (A fictional mystery to be release in Fall 2013) In a town possessed by "the flickering" that comes and goes twice every year, a local kid named Billy sets out to uncover just who is behind this haunting. Joined by his cousin, Cassie, this duo soon discovers the harrowing legacy of the "Lamplighter". Aided by a vintage snitch and his mysterious old lantern, Billy and Cassie find themselves exploring a place once called the "Funny Farm" and end up evolving into ghost detectives.

*A TOWN UNTANGLED* (A non-fiction collection of tattles) No matter how mediocre or mundane, all hometowns have storied pasts. In one true tale after another, the forlorn and sometimes forbidden folklore of a familiar place now gets revealed. Be forewarned, that you will encounter organized crime, religious strife, environmental disaster, romantic heartbreak, cultural chaos, and communal calamity. Historically haphazard and politically incorrect, these intrepid accounts might raise a few hackles, foster a gaggle of goose bumps, and rekindle some awkward moments.

*GLIMPSE* (A non-fiction memoir) Profiling the real life saga of a genuine Charlie Brown, this telltale story is one episode after another of dashing and crashing through adversity. Altogether audacious and somewhat off-kilter, this incriminating adventure shares a candid glimpse into the "Good Grief!" reality of being the ongoing square peg in a round hole. As such, what now comes to light, are the extraordinary measures, taken by some of us, just for the sake of fitting in.

*PLAYIN' POSSUM* (A children's picture book) Within this story are two young possums named Penny and Patty, who are taught to adapt in differing situations, by learning from each other.